Khushwant Singh is India's best-known writer and columnist. He has been founder-editor of Yojana, and editor of the *Illustrated Weekly of India*, the *National Herald* and the *Hindustan Times*. He is the author of classics such as *Train to Pakistan, I Shall Not Hear the Nightingale, Delhi* and *The Company of Women*. *The Sunset Club*, first published by Penguin Books in 2010, was written when he was ninety-five. His non-fiction includes the classic two-volume *A History of the Sikhs*, a number of translations and works on Sikh religion and culture, Delhi, nature, current affairs and Urdu poetry. His autobiography, *Truth, Love and a Little Malice*, was published by Penguin Books in 2002.

Khushwant Singh was a member of Parliament from 1980 to 1986. He was awarded the Padma Bhushan in 1974, but returned the decoration in 1984 in protest against the storming of the Golden Temple in Amritsar by the Indian army. In 2007, he was awarded the Padma Vibhushan.

Among the other awards he has received are the Punjab Ratan, the Sulabh International award for the most honest Indian of the year, and honorary doctorates from several universities.

PRAISE FOR *THE SUNSET CLUB*

'Has a little bit of everything for everyone: religion, communal violence, the Babri Masjid, the freedom movement, Ghalib, Iqbal, even Tiger Woods and the Nano'—*Hindustan Times*

'It's the kind of book that few writers would attempt today—gentle and unambitious in scope, tender in its recollections . . . What it stands for is a life, and how that life has been lived'—*Business Standard*

'It is hilarious, realistic, open and scandalous'—Gursharan Kaur

'It's light but serious, touching but funny. Singh wrestles with our enigmatic national character, but despite the weighty subject-matter, his book isn't pretentious . . . much of the book is as likely to find common ground with the young as with the old'—*DNA Sunday*

Also by Khushwant Singh

THE SUNSET CLUB

Analects of the Year 2009

Khushwant Singh

RAVI DAYAL

PENGUIN BOOKS

PENGUIN BOOKS
Published by the Penguin Group
Penguin Books India Pvt. Ltd, 11 Community Centre, Panchsheel Park,
New Delhi 110 017, India
Penguin Group (USA) Inc., 375 Hudson Street, New York, New York 10014, USA
Penguin Group (Canada), 90 Eglinton Avenue East, Suite 700, Toronto,
Ontario, M4P 2Y3, Canada (a division of Pearson Penguin Canada Inc.)
Penguin Books Ltd, 80 Strand, London WC2R 0RL, England
Penguin Ireland, 25 St Stephen's Green, Dublin 2, Ireland
(a division of Penguin Books Ltd)
Penguin Group (Australia), 250 Camberwell Road, Camberwell,
Victoria 3124, Australia (a division of Pearson Australia Group Pty Ltd)
Penguin Group (NZ), 67 Apollo Drive, Rosedale, Auckland 0632,
New Zealand (a division of Pearson New Zealand Ltd)
Penguin Group (South Africa) (Pty) Ltd, 24 Sturdee Avenue, Rosebank,
Johannesburg 2196, South Africa

Penguin Books Ltd, Registered Offices: 80 Strand, London WC2R 0RL, England

First published by Ravi Dayal Publisher and Penguin Books India 2010
Published in Penguin Books 2011

Copyright © Khushwant Singh 2010

Page 217 is an extension of the copyright page.

All rights reserved

10 9 8 7 6 5 4 3 2 1

ISBN 9780143417798

Typeset in Dante MT by SURYA
Printed at Thomson Press India Ltd, New Delhi

For Reeta Devi of Tripura
Maharani of Sujan Singh Park
Delhi's own Mother Teresa

CONTENTS

APOLOGIA

I had no intention of writing this novel. I had turned ninety-five and was not sure I would be able to finish it. Having nothing to do I became restless. Then Sheela Reddy of *Outlook* magazine suggested I record memories of my dead friends about whom I talked so much. The idea germinated and I got down to doing so. I mixed facts with fantasy.

My readers may find what I've written to be in bad taste—unacceptable in polite society. So be it. I have never been known for politeness or propriety. If you are offended by some things in the book, cast it aside.

I wish to place on record my deep gratitude to Diya Kar Hazra and Nandini Mehta, my editors at Penguin Books, and to Lachhman Das and Rajinder Ganju who put my scrawl into readable shape.

I

LODHI GARDENS

My story begins on the afternoon of Monday, the 26th of January 2009, the 59th anniversary of the founding of the independent Indian Republic. Although India gained independence from the British on the 15th of August 1947, its leaders wisely decided that mid-August was too hot and humid for outdoor celebrations and late January was a better time of the year to do so. So they picked the 26th of January, the day they gave the country its new Constitution. They declared it a national holiday and named it Republic Day—Ganatantra Divas.

By the end of January, winter loosens its grip; by sunrise, foggy dawns turn into sunny mornings; the time for flowers and the calling of barbets is round the corner.

Republic Day is the biggest event in India's calendar. It is the only one celebrated throughout the country by all of India's communities—Hindus, Muslims, Christians, Buddhists, Sikhs, Jains and Parsis. In every state capital they have flag hoistings, and parades of troops, police and schoolchildren.

However, there is nothing to match the grand spectacle in the capital city, with its display of India's military might and cultural diversity. Tanks, armoured cars, rocket launchers roll by; cannons boom; massed squads of soldiers, sailors, airmen march past, dipping their swords in salute; cavalrymen mounted on camels and horses are followed by floats of different states highlighting their achievements, with folk dancers dancing round them. People start assembling from the early hours of dawn, to line up along both sides of Rajpath. This broad avenue runs from Rashtrapati Bhavan—the President's Palace—atop Raisina Hill, down the slope between the two huge Secretariat buildings, North and South Blocks, to the massive War Memorial Arch known as India Gate, which bears the names of Indian soldiers who fell in the First World War, the Third Afghan War in 1919, and the 1971 confrontation with neighbouring Pakistan. In the centre of India Gate burns a celestial flame all day and night, in honour of men who laid down their lives for their Motherland.

You may well ask why India, which prides itself as the land of Gandhi, the apostle of peace and non-violence, celebrates the national day with such a display of lethal arms and fighting prowess. The truth is, we Indians are full of contradictions: we preach peace to the world and prepare for war. We preach purity of mind, chastity and the virtues of celibacy; we are also obsessed with sex. That makes us interesting. However, we do make up for the vulgar display of arms by having a Beating Retreat ceremony on Vijay Chowk (Victory Square) facing the Secretariat buildings. Here massed bands of the Army, Navy and Air Force bear no arms but trumpets, flutes, clarinets, drums and bagpipes, and march up and down the Square. The function ends with bells ringing out Gandhi's favourite hymn, 'Abide with Me'. A day later, on the 30th of January, the day we murdered Gandhi, our leaders assemble at Rajghat where we cremated him, and strew flowers on a slab of black marble where we reduced him to ashes. That's the kind of people we are. And that is why we are interesting.

Let me get back to my story. Around noon, the parade on Rajpath is over and crowds begin to disperse. Some go to the nearby Purana Qila, the Old Fort, to picnic on the lawns and doze in the sun. There are other ancient monuments which provide similar space and quiet. The most popular of them is Lodhi Gardens. It is within easy walking distance from Rajpath, and has a vast variety of trees, birds and medieval monuments. It is perhaps the

most scenic historic park in India. At one time it was a
scatter of tombs and mosques in a village called Khairpur.
In the 1930s the villagers were moved out and the monuments
taken under government protection.

Then the Vicereine, Lady Willingdon, who was
somewhat batty and wanted her name to go down in
posterity, had the scattered monuments enclosed within
walls and an entrance gate erected on the north side,
bearing the inscription 'Lady Willingdon Park'. She also
had a cinder track laid out for the Sahibs and their Mems
to ride on. All that is history. No one now calls it Lady
Willingdon Park, the cinder track has become a cobbled
stone footpath, and the park is known as Lodhi Gardens
because most of its monuments were built during the rule
of the Lodhi dynasty. Today it has three more entrances. A
second one is also in the north, with a small car park. People
have to walk across an old stone bridge called *aathpula*
(eight-spanned), over a moat which once guarded the walled
enclosure of the tomb of Sikandar Lodhi, built in 1518,
through an avenue of maulsari trees to the centre of the
park. There is another entrance on the eastern side, along
the India International Centre, and one more in the south,
close to a palm-lined avenue leading to the oldest tomb in
the complex, that of Muhammad Shah Sayyid, built in 1450.

For good reason, the most popular place in the park is
the extensive lawn on the southern side of what must

have been the main mosque, the Jami Masjid, built in 1494. The reason for its popularity is its dome, which is an exact replica of a young woman's bosom including the areola and the nipple. Most mosques and mausolea have domes but they have metal spires put on top of them which rob them of their feminine charm. Not the Bara Gumbad, the Big Dome. You can gape at it for hours on end and marvel at its likeness to a virgin's breast. You will notice that men sprawled on the lawns have their face towards it; their womenfolk sit facing the other way. It also has a bench facing it. Regular visitors to the park call it Boorha Binch, old men's bench, because for years, three old men have been sitting on it after they have hobbled round the park. While they talk, their gaze is fixed on Bara Gumbad. English-speaking Indians call them the 'Sunset Club' because the three men who occupy the bench are seen on it every day at sunset. All three are in their late eighties, the sunset years of their lives.

Let me introduce you to the members of the Sunset Club. First Pandit Preetam Sharma, because he is the eldest of the three. He is a Punjabi Brahmin, an Oxford graduate who served as cultural counsellor in London and Paris and rose to the highest position in the Ministry of

Education before he retired. He is well preserved, bald in front but with white locks flowing down his skull and curling up around his shoulders. They give him a scholarly look. He is in good health but needs glasses to read, hearing aids to hear and dentures to eat. He believes in Ayurveda and homeopathy. Although there were a succession of women, foreign and Indian, in his life, he narrowly escaped marrying one. He lives with his spinster sister, Sunita, who is almost twenty years younger than him and works with an NGO. They live in a ground-floor flat close to Khan Market. It has two bedrooms and two bathrooms, a large drawing–dining room, a study and two verandas.

One wall of the drawing room has a bookshelf packed with books which he has not read, nor intends to read. They create the impression that he is a man of learning. Other walls have paintings he made after he retired from service. No one except he understands what they are about but they do create the impression that he is a man of culture. He writes long poems in blank verse. He has them printed in Khan Market and gives copies freely to his visitors. Having risen to the top in the Ministry of Education, he is chairman of many cultural and social organizations and school boards. He makes a very good chairman as he makes profound statements like 'Culture knows no frontiers; all religions teach truth and love'; etc., etc. He has no enemies. All the men and women who know him love him. For company he has had a succession of Apsos named Dabboo One, Two and Three. He has a car and a chauffeur provided by a school whose chairman he is. It takes him, his servant Pavan and Dabboo Three to the northern entrance of Lodhi Gardens. He does a round of the park followed by Pavan and the dog before he takes his seat on the Boorha Binch. His servant and dog sit behind him on the lawn.

Second is Nawab Barkatullah Baig Dehlavi. He is a Sunni Mussalman whose Pathan ancestors settled in Delhi before the British took over the country. They combined soldiering with the practice of Yunani (Greek) medicine. They were granted land close to what is today Nizamuddin. Barkatullah's father set up a chain of Yunani *dawakhanas* (pharmacies) in the old city but preferred living in his large house in Nizamuddin. It is a spacious mansion named Baig Manzil. It has many rooms, verandas, a large garden in front and staff quarters at the back. Baig does not believe in amassing books; he finished with them after school and college. He has a few *diwans* of Urdu poets and an impressive collection of artefacts from Mughal times which are on display in his sitting room. He is a powerfully built six-footer with grey-white hair, a handlebar moustache and a short clipped beard.

Like all good Muslims from well-to-do families, Baig went to Aligarh Muslim University before he took over his father's business and, on his demise, his mansion. He is married to his cousin Sakina. They have a brood of children. But for occasional visits to Chawri Bazaar, the courtesans' street, and bedding his wife's maidservants in his younger days, he has been a faithful husband. After the partition of the country in 1947, he stayed on in India, joined the Congress Party and is a supporter of the Nehru–Gandhi dynasty. For over forty years he has been a regular stroller in Lodhi Gardens. The chauffeur of his Mercedes-Benz drops him at the southern entrance of the park. He does his rounds of the monuments followed by a servant pushing a wheelchair, before he takes his seat on the bench facing Bara Gumbad. Even in his eighties, Baig is in good shape: no glasses, no hearing aids, no false teeth, though he is occasionally short of breath.

Third is Sardar Boota Singh. He is a stocky Sikh with a paunch. The unshorn hair on his head is snow-white. Instead of tying a six-yard-long turban he has taken to wearing a cotton or woollen cap. He dyes his beard and looks younger than his eighty-six years. He suffers from many ailments: chronic constipation, incipient diabetes, fluctuating blood pressure, enlarged prostate and periodic bouts of gout. He has been wearing glasses since his schooldays, half a denture as all his lower teeth are gone, and for some years, hearing aids as well. He professes to be an agnostic sybarite, but every morning when he gets up around 4 a.m. he prays for his health and repeats *Aum Arogyam* many times, followed by the Gayatri Mantra and a Sikh hymn designed to keep sorrows at a distance:

May ill-winds not touch me, the Lord is my Protector.
Around me Rama has drawn a wall to protect me;
No harm will come to me, brother.
The True Guru, who put the Universe together
Gave me Rama's name as panacea against all ills;
Meditate on Him and Him alone.
He saves those who deserve saving; He removes all doubts
Says Nanak, the Lord is merciful. He is my helper.

He explains the contradictions in his agnosticism and hedonism by saying: 'Who knows! They say prayers can work miracles. No harm in trying them out.'

Prayers seldom help him, so he supplements them with a variety of pills from dawn to after dinner.

Boota had his higher education in England and served with Indian missions in London and Paris before he returned to Delhi and took to writing for newspapers. He lives in a flat close to Sharma's. The walls of his sitting room are lined with books: works of fiction, anthologies of poetry, biographies and books banned as pornographic. His favourites are books of quotations and anthologies of poetry, both Urdu and English. He has memorized quite a few and comes out with them at every opportunity. People think he is a man of learning but he knows he is a bit of a fraud.

Boota is a widower with two children. His son has migrated to Canada. His daughter, who is widowed, lives close by with her daughter. Though he lives alone, he is never lonely; he has a constant stream of ladies visiting him in the evening when he opens his bar. He is a great talker and a windbag. He makes up salacious stories of his conquests, which keep his audience spellbound. He uses bad language as if it was his birthright. When he is tired of company, he simply says, 'Now bugger off.' If he disapproves of a person, he calls him *'phuddoo'*, which is Punjabi for fucker. And every other person including himself is a *'chootia'*—cunt-born. Every evening he drives down to the India International Centre. He spends an hour there sipping coffee, then enters Lodhi Gardens through its eastern entrance past the Kos Minar. He too takes a couple of rounds of the park before he joins the other two on the bench facing Bara Gumbad.

How the three men got to form the Sunset Club is a long story. Sharma and Boota knew each other since their days in Lahore; by coincidence, both happened to be posted in London and then Paris at the same time. Back in Delhi both met in Lodhi Gardens every evening. Sharma was interested in meeting important people, Boota in trees and birds. Baig did not know either of them. For years he passed them as he did others. After some time they began to raise their hands in recognition. And still later, when they found themselves sitting on the same bench, introductions were made. They became friends and the Sunset Club came into being.

On the afternoon of the 26th of January 2009, Lodhi Gardens is more crowded than on other days. On its many lawns men and women lie sprawled on the grass. Around each group is a debris of paper plates and cups, with stray dogs wagging their tails, begging for leftovers.

One after another the three members of the Sunset Club arrive and take their seats on the Boorha Binch. Each one in turn puts out both hands with palms open as if pushing something—an all-India gesture asking if all is hunky-dory. After they have greeted each other with *aji aao* (come, come), *sab theek thaak* (is all okay?), Sharma replies: '*Bhagwan ki daya hai*—God is merciful.' Baig says: '*Alhamdulillah*—Allah be praised.' Boota says: '*Chalta hai*— life goes on.' Baig opens the dialogue: '*Ganatantra Divas mubarak ho*—congratulations for Republic Day.' Sharma returns the greetings in the same words: '*Aap ko bhi mubarak ho.*' Boota strikes a sour note: 'What is there to be congratulated about? We have made a bloody mess of our country. Murders, massacres, rapes, corruption, robberies like nothing we have ever seen before. Shame on us.'

Baig changes the subject. 'Did you watch the parade on TV? I never miss it.'

'Nor do I,' says Sharma. 'Grand display. Makes you feel proud of being Indian.'

'It is the same thing year after year, crores of rupees down the Yamuna,' snarls Boota.

'It is not the same year after year,' protests Baig. 'This is the first time our prime minister was unable to attend as he was in hospital after heart surgery. It is the first time we have had the president of Kazakhstan as our honoured guest.'

'Did you notice how bored he looked?' asks Boota. 'Most of the time he had his eyes shut as if falling off to sleep.'

'*Arrey bhai,*' protests Baig, 'he did not have his eyes shut. He is Mongoloid; they have narrow eyes like the Chinese.'

'Boota, does it never occur to you that this is one event in the year that everyone across the country watches every year? It generates a feeling of oneness in people of diverse religions, languages and races,' says Sharma raising his voice.

'Okay, okay bhai, you win. Two against one. Happy Ganatantra Divas to both of you,' responds Boota in a voice loaded with sarcasm.

'So what's new?' asks Baig.

'What's new is that last night I had a wet dream. You are a *hakeem*. I wanted to ask you if it is okay for a man of my age to have wet dreams.'

Before Baig can reply Sharma breaks in: 'That's because you have dirty thoughts. What you can't do, you imagine you are doing. I bet you can't even get an erection any more. Anyhow, who was it who wet your pajamas?'

'I won't tell you. You know her very well. And I sought Hakeem Sahib's opinion, not yours,' Boota snaps back.

Baig ponders over the matter before he replies, 'You must be constipated. Constipation often induces night discharge of semen.'

Boota is taken aback. 'I've always had problems with my stomach. I have been taking laxatives since I left college.'

'You have a problem of gas in the stomach?' asks Baig.

'Yes, lots. I can't do anything about it.'

Boota tells Baig only half the truth. The truth is that Boota does not want to do anything about it because he enjoys farting. His wife's death relieved him from the bondage of good manners. When alone, he lets himself go—bhoom, phatas, phuss. And he revels in inhaling the stink he produces. 'My stomach is full of gas till the evening. When I take Scotch it seems to subside,' he adds.

'I don't like telling you this, but you could not have been a great performer. People who have gas problems don't make great lovers. They rarely succeed in bringing a woman to her climax. Am I right?'

Boota winces. He recalls that in his earlier years in college in England, he often came in his trousers while kissing girls passionately. Even later it was only when he was a little drunk that he lasted fifteen to twenty minutes, and once in a while brought a woman to a climax.

'Talk about something else,' says Sharma. 'Don't always have sex on your mind. It's bad for your health, particularly when you are old and can't do anything.'

'Okay bhai, we will postpone it till tomorrow evening. Let's talk about God and life hereafter of which we know nothing,' replies Boota.

By that time the sun has gone down behind Bara Gumbad. It has begun to turn chilly. Lights on footpaths have been switched on, Bara Gumbad lit up. Baig's servant puts a shawl on his master's lap. 'Sahib, it is getting cold. We better go home,' he says in a tone of authority. 'See, most people have already left.'

All three get up. Sharma says, 'Cheerio,' Boota says, 'Sleep well,' Baig says, '*Allah Hafiz*—God protect you.' They go back the way they came.

∾

Sharma gets back to his ground-floor apartment followed by Dabboo Three and his servant. Dabboo Three announces their return with a couple of barks, Sharma's sister Sunita lets them in with her usual words of welcome: 'You are back.' Sharma makes no response. He puts his walking stick in its usual corner and sits down in his padded armchair. There is a roaring log fire in the grate—he likes to keep warm. His servant takes off his shoes and slips his woollen bedroom slippers on to his feet.

'Who-who was there?' asks Sunita.

Sharma's temper rises. 'How many times have I told you not to say who-who? One who is enough.'

Sunita protests, 'I did not go to Balliol. I was in Hindu College. Who-who for *kaun-kaun*. What is so wrong with it?'

'It is not English and when speaking English, use English; when speaking Hindi, speak Hindi. Don't make a *khichdi* of both.'

'*Achha bhai*, who was there?'

'Boota and Baig.'

'What did you talk about?'

'This and that.'

Sunita senses he is not in a mood to talk to her. 'I hope that Boota does not barge in. He is always one for a free drink. He also uses dirty language. His servant says he doesn't bathe for two-two, three-three days. He must smell.'

'Again two-two, three-three days! You will never learn.'

Sunita decides to end the debate. 'You take it from me, this is the kind of English we Indians will speak—Hinglish.'

Pavan pours out whisky, soda and two cubes of ice in a tumbler and places it on the side table beside his master's chair. A bowl of peanuts is already there. Sunita turns her back and joins the servants, their wives and children to watch a serial on Zee TV.

Sharma takes a couple of sips of whisky–soda, stretches his legs and shuts his eyes. He goes over Baig's analysis of Boota's wet dream. He has never suffered from constipation. As a matter of fact, he often boasted to Boota how his stomach worked like clockwork: two motions every morning, one before and another after breakfast. Every time, he announced it to everyone around in French, using two words he had picked up in his six years spent in Paris: *deuxieme fois*—second time. And yet, his first intimate contact with a female was little short of a disaster. It was monsoon time. He was later than usual working in his office to dispose of some urgent files to be sent to his minister. By the time he finished, it was dark. As he was leaving the Secretariat building he saw one of his lady deputy secretaries in the crowd, waiting for the rain to stop. He had often exchanged flirtatious dialogue with her.

'Lakshmi, can I give you a lift? It's drizzling,' he asked. She beamed a smile and replied, 'Please. I don't want to get drenched.' A chaprasi opened his umbrella and escorted the two to Sharma's office car. Sharma was tired. He sat with his legs stretched and his right arm resting on the back of the seat above Lakshmi's head. By accident his arm fell on her shoulder. She turned her face to him and kissed him on his lips. He was taken aback but responded passionately. They kept their lips glued together for a long time. He got a hard erection. He could not hold back and slipped his hand up to the middle of her thighs. 'Not today,' she whispered, 'I am not well. I have my periods.' He did not know anything about periods and thought she was making excuses. He pushed his hand further, found a padded obstruction, oozing blood. 'I told you so, darling. Be patient. You can have as much of it as you like after we are married.'

That is as close as Sharma ever got to having sex. Later in the evening he went to consult Boota on the subject. 'I thought she was making excuses to keep me off till I marry her. But she was really wounded and bleeding.' The only comment Boota made on his friend's misadventure was, 'Phuddoo! Chootia! How old are you?'

Sharma feels drowsy, his head droops on his chest. Sunita notices it and asks, 'Will you eat here or at the table?'

'Here.'

His servant brings a bowl of boiled rice, dal, a couple of karelas, and puts the food beside the bowl of peanuts. Sharma does not relish the food his sister gives him but has stopped complaining, because she then reminds him of the adage he often uses—'simple living, high thinking'. So she gives him a tasteless but belly-filling *bhojan*. Sharma gulps down the whisky, gobbles up the food, goes to the bathroom to rinse his mouth, urinates and goes to bed. His evenings have become deadly boring.

Boota returns home to a brightly lit fire, his single malt whisky, soda and bucket of ice cubes on a tray. He pours himself a double Patiala in a crystal cut-glass tumbler he uses only for himself, adds ice and soda. He munches some wasabi peas and cashewnuts, then fills his mouth with whisky and rolls it round with his tongue before letting it trickle down his throat. He wants to see if he can feel it go down to his intestines. When his stomach is clean, he can; when it is not, he cannot. He switches on the TV for a few minutes, watches cheetahs chasing deer, and some Australian wrestling with crocodiles and pythons, then switches it off, shuts his eyes and lets his mind drift back to his affairs with women in his younger days. He was never a great performer but the variety he performed with is impressive: whites, browns, blacks, Canadians, Americans, Germans, French, and of course Indians from all communities and parts of the country: Christians, Jews, Hindus, Muslims, Sikhs. Only a few encounters have stayed in his mind, others have faded from his memory.

One, particularly, keeps repeating itself. He was staying with friends in England. They had a young, attractive, English governess for their daughter. It was Christmas time. His hosts and their daughter had gone calling on friends. He was lying on a sofa when the governess brought him a glass of sherry. They exchanged 'Merry Christmas' greetings with light kisses on each other's cheeks. That was the prelude. The hosts returned with a couple of their friends for the Christmas feast—roast turkey, French wine, pudding loaded with rum, followed by cognac and Drambuie. Everyone was a little tipsy by the end of the evening. He bade them goodnight and returned to his bedroom on the top floor, which was next to that of the governess. Some minutes later he heard her footsteps going into her bedroom. Sleep would not come to him. He tiptoed to her bedroom. She made room for him as if expecting him. He laid himself on her and glued his lips to hers. She opened her thighs to let him in. He entered her. They lay in silence for what seemed like divine eternity. At long last he came with violent jerks and pumped half a gallon of his semen into her without bothering about the consequences. Mercifully there were none. He concluded that those who found English women cold had never sampled one. They continued to meet in different places and made love every time.

Boota's wife had kept an excellent table. She consulted a lot of cookery books: French, Italian, Chinese and

Indian. She spent a good half-hour instructing the cook how to go about preparing various recipes. He turned out to be a master craftsman in the art of cooking. She had gone eight years ago but the cook was still with him and gave him a gourmet dinner every evening. Boota relishes good food, a glass of French wine, followed by a digestive Underberg. He swallows a dozen pills prescribed for his age for various ailments. Then he switches off for the night. He sleeps fitfully as he has to get up two or three times to empty his bladder. Nevertheless, he is up by 4 a.m. to start the day's work.

By the time Baig's Mercedes-Benz gets to Nizamuddin, street lights have been switched on. Hazrat Nizamuddin's shrine, which allows worshippers of all communities, has in its complex tombs of the poets Amir Khusrau and Mirza Ghalib, as well as bazaars all around, which attract large crowds. Baig's car leaves the main Delhi–Agra road to enter the elite residential area, Nizamuddin West. The headlights of his car catch the two marble slabs on either side of the gates. One in English reads 'Baig Manzil', the other in Arabic 'Hada bin Fazl-e-Rabbee—this by the Grace of God'. On top of the house is a circular marble slab with the numerals 786 in Arabic. God has certainly been good to the Baig family. The double-storeyed mansion is brightly lit. People refer to it as Baig's *daulat khana*—abode of wealth; he calls it *ghareeb khana*—house of poverty.

Begum Sakina awaits him in the veranda. He is helped to his armchair in the sitting room. A coal fire is glowing, his armchair has a small pillow to cushion his large frame, a *moorha* (cane stool) in front to rest his feet, a bottle of Black Label Scotch, a tumbler, ice bucket and a plate of shaami kababs on the side table. Sakina Begum sees him settle down comfortably, orders two of her maids to press his legs and retires to the neighbouring room from where she can see him as well as the *saas–bahu* TV serials to which she is addicted. She does not approve of his drinking as the Koran forbids consumption of alcohol to Muslims. But she refrains from reminding her husband about it.

Baig pours himself a generous peg; his servant adds soda and two cubes of ice. He takes a big swig of the whisky–soda, bits of shaami kabab, and stretches his legs out on the moorha. The maids sit on their haunches on either side of the moorha and begin to press his legs. That's all they do during the day for the Begum Sahiba and have become expert masseuses. First his feet. They press the insteps with their thumbs; then by turn every toe with their thumbs and index fingers. Then his legs with their palms. And back to his feet. They do not stop till told to do so. Baig is transported to another world.

What more would he get in paradise than good Scotch and houris pressing his limbs: Paradise is a man-made fantasy; this is for real. He recalls Mirza Ghalib's lines: 'We know the truth about Paradise: it is a good idea to beguile the mind.' However, he knows that these pleasures will also not last very long as old age robs life of the fun of living.

Ghalib was a man after Baig's own heart: hard drinker, lover of women, only prayed on Fridays, never fasted during Ramadan. And yet, not only Muslims but all Urdu-knowing people of the world swear by his name as one of the greatest poets of all time. Baig recalls one of his favourite Ghalib couplets:

Where are the frivolities of yesteryear?
Where has your youth fled?

Where indeed had his youth fled? He recalled the early days of his married life. He was eighteen, Sakina sixteen. They had played together as children, teased each other in their early teens. He had noticed her bosom take shape and her buttocks get rounder. They had got down to real business on the first night they were left alone. She had called him Barkoo Bhaiyya and he had called her Sakki. Overnight, he became Janoo—sweetheart—and she became Begum.

What a volcano of passion she had in her little frame! They were at it every time they were on their own—at times, six times in one day. She found him too heavy and suggested she come on top. He found that even pleasanter and lay on his back with his massive circumcised penis up like the Qutub Minar. She mounted him, directed his erect member inside her till it disappeared between her thighs. She did most of the work, kissing his eyes, his lips, heaving up and down. It was her groaning with ecstasy that brought him to a climax. What bliss it was! As expected, she was pregnant by the second month. She had morning sickness and went back to her parents for a week's break.

That was too long for Baig. Sex had become compulsive. So he took her maids to bed in turn: one when she brought his early morning cup of tea, the other when she brought him the glass of hot milk he took before retiring for the night. The girls took it as a part of their duty. He didn't have any qualms of conscience. He repeated the exercise whenever his wife was far gone in her pregnancy and went to her parents for the delivery.

Occasionally he visited courtesans in Chawri Bazaar to watch their *mujra* and dance. The evening ended with his having sex with one of them. He tipped them handsomely. Sakina had a woman's sixth sense about her husband's infidelities but never questioned him. As long as he did not bring in a second wife, it was okay by her. That was the way of nawabs, rajas and rich businessmen. He was both a nawab and a man of substance.

Baig's reverie is disturbed by his wife's gentle query, 'Khana?'

'*Haan*,' he mumbles in reply.

Whisky, soda and tumbler are removed along with the side table. A larger table is brought with a couple of plates on it. Sakina Begum joins him.

'What was the *gup-shup* about this evening?' she asks.

'Not for your ears, Begum. That Sardar uses language not proper in polite society. Most of it is about his exploits with women.'

'*Chheeh! Chheeh!* Why do you talk to him?'

'He can be quite entertaining. Knows a lot of Urdu poetry.'

Dinner is laid on the table by a relay of servants: mutton biryani flavoured with saffron, three kinds of mutton and chicken curries, baghaara baigan (aubergines cooked in Hyderabadi style), chapattis and naans. Every night it is a royal feast. Sakina piles biryani on his plate till he says '*bas*—enough'. Mutton curry? Chicken curry? She heaps his plate till he raises his hand to say no more. Sakina spreads a napkin on his lap and hands him his plate. He waits for her to fill her plate and sit down. '*Bismillah*,' he intones. They eat with their fingers: spoons and forks rob food of its taste.

Every evening large quantities of food are removed from the table. It is never wasted because the entire staff of six servants and their families are fed. So are beggars from Nizamuddin who cluster round the entrance gate. For dessert there is phirni covered with silver *varq* in an earthen cup, kulfi, ice cream and a variety of fruits of the season. Both take phirni—this time scooped up with spoons. The fruit goes untouched.

A servant brings a jug of warm water, soap, towels and a basin. They wash their hands, rinse their mouths and spit the contents into the basin. Baig lets out a loud *dakar* (belch) to express thanks for the delicious meal. The servants remove the table and put back the side table with a box of Romeo y Julieta cigars, clipper and lighter on it. Baig clips the end of his cigar and lights it. Sakina disapproves of smoking as much as of drinking, and quietly retires to another room.

It takes nearly half an hour for Baig to finish his Havana cigar, each costing around five hundred rupees. It is worth every paisa as it gives him time to digest his dinner. He tosses the butt into the grate of dying embers and growls '*chalo*—let's go'. Two servants help him go to the bathroom to brush his teeth, urinate, change into his night kurta-pajama and get on his bed. He takes two pinches of digestive *chooran* made of pomegranate seeds. He switches on his table lamp, reads a few couplets of Ghalib which he knows by heart. By then he is heavy with sleep. He switches off the table lamp, lays his head down on his pillow and begins to snore. That is one reason Sakina has given up sharing his bedroom. She sleeps in the next room where her husband's snoring does not disturb her, yet assures her all is well with the world.

The outside lights are kept lit throughout the night. The chowkidar keeps strolling between the entrance and exit gates, thumping his lathi on the tarmac surface, *thak-thak*, shouting periodically *Khabardar raho*—remain alert!

~

For old people, mornings are an ordeal. No matter what age-related ailments they suffer from, it is usually in the mornings from sunrise to noon that they succumb to them. More old people die during these hours than at others. This is a blessing in disguise as in tropical climates relatives dispose of their dead before sunset. And many deaths are related to bowel movements because they weigh heavily on their minds. Some have to strain at their stools, which takes a toll on their hearts. Others have breathing problems and are short of breath; their exertions on the commode also strain the heart till it gives way.

Though Sharma never had problems with his bowels he had an enlarged prostate which blocked his urine. Medical examination showed early stages of cancer. He was operated on in good time. He got rid of the cancer but it made his bladder uncontrollable. He has to get up twice or thrice at night to empty it in the pisspot that is kept under his bed.

Boota Singh is bowel-obsessed. He takes laxatives, enemas, glycerine suppositories up his rectum. For the last few years he has been taking three heaped teaspoonfuls of Isabgol in a glass of warm milk every morning. Sometimes he has a good clearance. But more often nothing works.

Baig, though he eats richer food, takes little exercise, and is overweight, has no complaint about his bowels.

ॐ

Sharma gets up after daylight, stretches out his arms and loudly intones *Hari Om Tat Sat* a few times, coming down to just *Hari Om, Hari Om*. He goes to the bathroom to urinate and rinse his mouth. Then he downs a tumbler of warm water and a mug of tea. He goes on to recite the Gayatri Mantra at the top of his voice:

Almighty God: Creator of the Earth and the firmament
Blessed be Thy Name
And blessed be the Sun that gives us light and life
May thou endow me with similar qualities
May such thoughts enlighten my mind.

He waits for a few minutes till pressure builds up in his bowels. Thereafter he has his bath and gets into fresh clothes. He has a good breakfast of cereal, a couple of fried eggs, and is ready to face the day. He does not believe in subscribing to newspapers as he can read them all in the library of the India International Centre. Soon after his sister leaves for her office, his driver takes him to the Centre. He spends his mornings there, has a bite in the coffee lounge and returns home for a long siesta.

For Boota mornings are, as he says, a pain in the arse. He is up before 4 a.m. He swallows a couple of pills with a tumbler of orange juice. He sits down on a well-cushioned armchair. He says he does not believe in prayer but he prays for his bowels to move smoothly: 'Aum Arogyam.' He repeats the mantra many times. He keeps looking at the three table clocks in his bedroom and his pocket watch lying on the table. He looks through the window to see if dawn has come. From 5.30 a.m. newspapers start arriving. He subscribes to six. In the *Hindustan Times* and the *Times of India* he only reads the headlines and turns the pages of their supplements to see the tits and bums of Bollywood starlets. His morning preoccupation is solving crossword puzzles. With breakfast of a tumbler of warm milk with Isabgol he takes eight more pills prescribed for his fluctuating blood pressure, enlarged prostate, wind in the stomach and other age-related ailments. If his fake prayers and the pills do what they are meant to and he succeeds in filling the toilet bowl with his shit, he hears koels calling from the mango groves. If not, it is the kaw-kaw of crows all day long.

Baig's household are early risers. As the call for the Fajr prayer, *Allah-o-Akbar*, wafts across from the mosque in Nizamuddin, Begum Sakina and all the servants turn towards Makka, raise their hands to their ears and offer namaaz. Nawab Sahib's day begins much later. He announces it by stretching his arms wide with a loud cry, 'Ya Allah.' It is a signal for the household to get down to their daily chores. He goes to the bathroom to urinate and rinse his mouth. As he sits in his armchair by the fireplace, Sakina joins him with the greeting, '*Salaam Alaikum. Did you sleep well?*' He replies: '*Valaikum Salaam.* Allah be praised, I slept soundly.' A servant greets his master likewise, brings a silver tray with two Spode china cups on saucers, with silver spoons, a bowl of sugar cubes and a silver teapot covered by a tea cosy to keep it hot. Sakina pours tea, milk and sugar in the two cups, and hands one to her husband. She takes her seat with cup in hand. 'What is the programme for the day?' she asks.

'The same,' he replies, 'Some business, meeting people, eating the air in Lodhi Gardens and back home. Comes the morning, comes the evening and the day is done. This is the way in which our lives end.'

The tea tray is removed. Another servant brings an ornate silver hookah with an earthenware bowl full of live embers and fragrant tobacco. Baig takes a few pulls and utters a loud 'ah' at the end of each puff. A few puffs of his hookah is all he needs to activate his bowels. He doesn't care a fig about what goes on in the world. He gets one English paper, the *Hindustan Times*, for no better reason than that his father used to get it. He scans the headlines and the obituary columns and puts it aside. He used to subscribe to the Urdu journal, *Qaumi Awaaz*. Since it closed down, he gets *Roznama Rashtriya Sahara*, *Hindustan Express* and *Sahafat*. Also several magazines— *Nai Duniya*, *Sahara Times* and *Pakeeza Aanchal*. He never reads any of them; Begum Sakina goes over every one of them before she passes them on to her servants, all of whom can read Urdu. Baig gets his news second-hand from his wife, with suitable comments: *Besharam!* (shameless), *Goonda kahin ka!* (no-good thug), *Naalaik* (stupid) or just *Thoo!* Her *wah-wahs* are reserved for tennis star Sania Mirza and Muslims in India's Cricket Eleven.

Members of the Sunset Club do not normally meet on the evening of Beating Retreat. All three watch the spectacle on their TV sets. This year it was cancelled as a mark of respect for ex-President Venkataraman who had died two days earlier—all public ceremonies were cancelled for eleven days and flags flown at half-mast.

Indians have enormous respect for the dead. If the head clerk of an office dies, the entire office staff takes the day off. They have different ways of expressing their grief. Some take their families to the cinema, others take them to the zoo or for picnics to the Qutub Minar or to Okhla, where there is a barrage from where the Yamuna canal takes off. The next day they have a meeting. The boss makes a short speech, extolling the qualities of head and heart of their departed colleague. They stand in silence for a minute with their heads lowered. Then they go back to their desks and shuffle files, drink relays of tea or coffee. And gossip.

That afternoon there were lots of picnickers in Lodhi Gardens. As they took their seats, Baig remarked, 'There is a lot of *raunaq* in the garden today.'

'Has to be,' says Boota, 'Venkataraman died the day before yesterday. So there have to be *shok sabhas*—condolence meetings. This is as nice a place as any to hold one. Let's forget Venkataraman. What do you make of the Chandra Mohan–Anuradha affair in Chandigarh? The papers are full of it.'

Sharma is the first to answer: 'Shameful! A Brahmin girl from a respectable family marrying a married fellow with two children. And a Bishnoi at that. The founder of the sect, Guru Jambeshwar, was a noble soul, a visionary, a century ahead of his time, the first environmentalist.

Don't kill trees, don't kill animals, don't hurt people, don't tell lies—that's what he preached. He even sanctioned selecting handsome, healthy males to service married women whose husbands could not impregnate them. That's the reason why the Bishnois are a handsome people. And see what happened to them. At one time the British intended to declare them a criminal tribe. They have a very high rate of murders and violent crimes. And we had this fellow's father Bhajan Lal who was once chief minister of Haryana. Overnight he changed sides and bribed MLAs to join him. Now his son has gone one better than his father—he deserts his family to have illicit relations with an upper-caste woman.'

Baig speaks next. 'Sharmaji, there is nothing Bishnoi or Brahmin about it. Love crosses all barriers of race, religion, caste, wealth and poverty. Mirza Ghalib's lines on *ishq*— love—say it best:

No power can hold it back; it is a fire
When you try to ignite it, it refuses to ignite,
When you want to put it out, it refuses to be put out.

'Ishq-vishq, love-shove, all bullshit,' Boota cuts in. 'Baig Sahib, lust is real, love is the gloss romantics put on it. Lust is natural. It begins to build up in infancy, assumes compelling proportions in adolescence, and lasts till old age. Boys start getting erections and want to put them in other boys' bottoms or girls' bums; girls start getting damp in their middles. Nature compels all of them to put their thighs together, fuck away till they are spent. Let me tell you what probably passed between the Bishnoi and the Brahmini. The Bishnoi wanted a new woman and was on the prowl, looking for a dainty dish. The Brahmini in her mid-thirties, fair-skinned, black curly hair hanging down to her shoulders, eyes of a gazelle, bosom like this Bara Gumbad in front of us. Their eyes meet. Lust is aroused. So they get down to the act: *Tamaam shud*— that's all.'

'Bhai Boota, no one can answer you,' protests Baig with a smile. 'You get down to the basics. Don't forget that love, not lust, has generated the greatest poetry in all languages of the world.'

Sharma cuts in impatiently: 'Forget love and lust, aren't you concerned about the harm such illicit liaisons do to society? A married man with a family and also deputy chief minister of Haryana should be setting an example in propriety. And that woman, a lawyer, advises him that the easiest way to avoid being charged with bigamy, which is a crime, is to convert to Islam which sanctions bigamy. Disgraceful!'

Baig is not one to let Sharma get away with a slur on Islam. 'Sharma Sahib, Islam does not sanction bigamy; it permits it if a marriage does not work out. You must know a lot of Muslims: can you name even one who has more than one wife? I can name several Hindus in important positions—chief ministers of states, MPs, film stars, dancers, business tycoons. Not one has been prosecuted for bigamy. Nevertheless, everyone blames Muslims for being bigamous. Here am I, who finds it hard enough to cope with one wife!'

'I am sorry if I hurt your feelings. But you take it from me that the Chandra Mohan–Anuradha drama is not yet over. There will be lots of ups and downs in the time to come.'

'I agree,' says Boota, slapping his thighs loudly with both hands. 'We are a people full of contradictions. On one side we have a couple who break all rules of propriety, on the other we have fundoos like those of the Ram Sene in Mangalore who beat up boys and girls for drinking beer in a pub. These goondas should be stripped naked and beaten with chappals on their bare bottoms. What do you say, Baig Sahib? You must have read about it in the papers.'

'Some people don't know how to mind their own business,' replies Baig. 'Unfortunately, we have lots of them in our country.'

'So you think we should ignore them or *joota maro* them? Spit on their bums before we smack their backside with chappals?'

Before they bid each other goodnight they generally allude to the subject uppermost in their minds; it is too delicate to be put bluntly. Baig quotes Ghalib:

> *Life goes at a galloping pace*
> *Where it will stop, no one knows;*
> *Our hands are not on the reins*
> *Our feet not in the stirrups.*

Boota adds another couplet:

> *There is a day fixed for death*
> *Why then spend sleepless nights thinking about it?*

Sharma says, 'Cheerio.'

On that happy note they bid each other farewell for the day.

2

THE MONTH OF

FLOWERS

The last day of January 2009 is Basant Panchami which, by the Indian Vikrami calendar, marks the end of winter and the advent of spring. The Vikrami calendar is closer to the change of seasons than the Roman calendar. There is a popular saying, *Aaya Basant, Paala udant*—comes Basant, the cold has flown. And indeed the short spring makes a colourful entry and melts in the summer's heat by the end of February. In the flatlands of northern India the mustard is in full flower. At places it is a sea of bright canary yellow. In honour of the mustard flower, men wear yellow turbans, women yellow dupattas.

North Indians, unlike Bengalis, are not great users of mustard oil or mustard seed. It is the mustard leaf that they consume with passion for weeks to come. The leaf is crushed, mixed with some other vegetable, seasoned with garlic and ginger and made into *sarson ka saag*—a puree made of mustard leaves. A blob of fresh butter is put on the green mash and ladled into the mouth with pieces of *bajra* (millet) or corn bread: it is a feast for kings.

Basant is also the time to fly kites. Indians have not experimented with making new designs and stick to the traditional square pattern of different colours. What is unique about kite-flying in India is that it has become a kind of warfare. Kite flyers resort to dirty tricks like coating strings with powdered glass which not only cuts the strings of other kites but the necks of people who have the misfortune of coming in their way; they also tangle with electric wires and cause short circuits. People get on their rooftops and send their kites soaring into the sky; they entwine with other kites and as soon as one is cut asunder and floats down in waves, triumphant cries of '*Bokata*' rent the heavens. Boys armed with long bamboo poles with spikes on top chase the vanquished kite and claim it as their war trophy.

February is Delhi's floral month. All parks and roundabouts are, as the cliché goes, a riot of colours. You can see the flowers at their best in Buddha Jayanti Park on the Ridge. There they have long flower beds growing the same flowers en masse. Lodhi Gardens cannot claim to provide such a feast for the eyes for flower-lovers. Undoubtedly, it has an enclosed rose garden with exotic varieties of roses which are beautiful to look at but lack fragrance. Few people besides rose-fanciers bother to visit it. There are a few nondescript flower beds on both sides of its footpaths, but Lodhi Gardens makes up by having an incredible variety of flowering trees which come into bloom in February. They attract lots of tree-lovers.

Members of the Sunset Club have their own reasons for preferring Lodhi Gardens to other city parks. As I said before, Sharma likes to exchange greetings with important people: members of Parliament, senior politicians and retired civil servants. Most of them recognize him because he is a retired important person. Baig has an abiding interest in ancient monuments, notably those built by Pathan kings who once ruled the whole of northern India. Lodhi Gardens reminds him of the glorious rule of the Sayyid and Lodhi Sultans. Boota Singh does not bother about VIPs nor is he very interested in monuments; he pretends to be a nature lover—birds and trees are what draw him to the park because it has lots of both.

His own attempts to grow exotic varieties of trees have not been very successful. Many years ago he brought a sandalwood sapling from Mysore. Boota didn't know it is a parasite and its roots feed on roots of trees nearby and turn the trunk into fragrant wood. It now stands twenty feet tall in his garden. But it has no fragrance. About the same time, he planted a hybrid Amrapali mango tree close to the sandalwood. It grew rapidly, had clusters of white *boor* flowers, of which a few turned into fruit which was inedible. He planted six avocados. They grew to respectable heights and then collapsed without bearing fruit.

About ten years ago he bought a sapling of what the nurseryman told him was a kadam and planted it close to his rear veranda. It has grown to over thirty feet. A most handsome tree, thick with large green leaves. Around the end of February it begins to shed its leaves and sprout new ones of bright orange colour. Boota watches it by the hour as its leaves start to drop. Gusts of wind bring some down in showers. And soon new ones turn the tree into a flowering pyramid of fire, a sight for the gods.

Boota invites friends over to see it. One of them came around with Pradip Krishen's book, *Trees of Delhi*. He had one look at the tree and said, 'This is not a kadam but a kosam.' And showed him the pictures and text in the book. A few days later he sent him a kadam sapling as a gift. Boota planted it in the middle of his garden. It is already over twenty feet high: one trunk, branches at regular intervals, large light green leaves—it is a balm for sore eyes. Boota has switched his affection from the kosam to the kadam.

In February, quite a few trees are in flower. At the western side of the lawn with the Boorha Binch are towering semuls—silk cotton—with large, ungainly red flowers, neither beautiful nor fragrant. Further down the lawn facing the tomb of Muhammad Shah Sayyid are a few dhaks, better known as palas, or flame of the forest. No one plants them in their own gardens because they have nothing to show for themselves except for the week or two when they are in flower. Their flowers last till the end of February or first week of March. You can see them growing wild in and around Buddha Jayanti Park. Apparently the battlefield on which Robert Clive got the better of Nawab Sirajuddowlah in 1757 had lots of them in full bloom and hence the battle came to be known as the Battle of Plassey, after palas. Its parrot-beak-shaped flowers are pretty to behold but have no scent. Behind Sheesh Gumbad, which is just west of the Bara Gumbad, there are a few coral trees. Their flowers are the same colour as the dhak but instead of being curved, are straight. Also without scent. It is these trees that are the focus of Boota's attention and he lectures about them to the other two members of the Sunset Club.

Boota is given to fantasizing when he is awake and dreaming when he is asleep. His fantasies and dreams have changed with the years. When he was young, he fantasized about young women he met and fancied. Often he had them in mind when he masturbated. He hoped they would reappear in his dreams and make them sweet. They never did: every time he had a wet dream it was about a woman he had never fantasized about. As he grew older, his fantasies became tinged with ambition and envy. He would score over his rivals, and receive recognition and applause when he reached the top.

His dreams also changed their pattern with age. When young he dreamt of flying unaided into space, then dropping with a thud which woke him up. Then followed insecurity dreams: finding himself taking an exam and being unable to answer a single question; being at a formal reception wearing only a *kachha* (underwear); losing his way, missing buses and trains; forgetting the number of his room in a hotel, having no money to pay the hotel bill. And that sort of thing. As he turned eighty, with an enlarged prostate and chronic constipation, both bladder and bowels became topics of his dreams. He dreamed of his bladder bursting to empty itself and not finding a place where he could do so in privacy; likewise he waited desperately to defecate, seated on a commode straining to get rid of a hard stool when somebody barged in. These became recurrent nightmares.

Boota is always a little sozzled by the time he switches off for the night. Yet he sleeps fitfully. He gets up twice or thrice every night to empty his bladder. Even so, he is up well before 4 a.m., and his mornings are preoccupied by asking himself, 'Will I or won't I be able to get a satisfactory clearance of bowels?' He goes over what he drank and ate the evening before. No more than one large single malt followed by scrambled egg on toast, and kulfi. Was his inside rotting faster than his brain? How long would the game last? After that, what? His mind and his body would part forever. All that might remain of them would be memories in the minds of people who knew him. The night of the 8th of February is worse than others. He is up before 3 a.m. and relaxes in his armchair, hoping to doze off for an hour or so. No luck. He gives up in disgust and decides to take an early morning walk. He has not done so for many years. It is still chilly enough for him to wear a sweater. He gets into his walking shoes, picks up the keys of his car and slips out of his flat quietly lest he disturb his servant who sleeps on the floor in the next room. It is still and silent. A full moon shines in all its glory, with the morning star sparkling near it. When was it he last saw the moon and the stars? The wretched city lights have robbed people of their right to darkness. Spotted owlets sitting in the mulberry trees greet him with chitter-chitter, chatter-chatter. When was it he last heard these birds greet him?

He drives down an empty road, reaches India International Centre and parks his car in the empty car park. He sits in the car till the grey light of dawn overtakes the moonlit sky. He walks past the Kos Minar. He is surprised to see the number of people in the park at this early hour. They seem to be in a hurry: some jogging, others walking at a brisk pace, no strollers, no talkers. Boota does two rounds before he sits down on the Boorha Binch to take in the morning scene. There are lots of people doing yoga—padma asan (lotus pose), dhanur asan (bow-like pose), shirsh asan (standing on their heads), or just taking long breaths through one nostril and exhaling loudly through the other. Why can't they do all this in their homes, wonders Boota. Why make an exhibition of themselves in public places?

More is to come. Around thirty middle-aged men and women, all looking glum as if they had recently lost their maternal grandmothers, form a semicircle in front of a man clad in a white khaddar kurta and dhoti. He raises both his arms to call for silence. He drops his arms with a jerk like a conductor ordering his orchestra to begin playing. He sets the tone with two loud 'ha-has'. They follow with loud ha-has hee-hees, ho-hos at different pitches. Some double up in an ecstasy of laughter, others throw up their arms in sheer joy. This goes on for almost ten minutes till they are exhausted. As they break up to return to their homes, they look more relaxed, some have smiles on their faces. This is the Laughter Club of Lodhi Gardens.

Boota mutters to himself: '*Khotey*—donkeys,' and lets his mind go back to the time when the Bara Gumbad was the city's principal mosque. He imagines the scene as it might have been in those days: the early morning call for Fajr namaaz, Allah-o-Akbar, would rise to the heavens; worshippers would line up and go through their genuflections, murmuring verses from the Koran. And then the imam would pause and ask angrily: 'Who are these infidel donkeys braying outside and disturbing us paying homage to our Maker? Off with their heads!' The Laughter Club of Lodhi Gardens would have had little left to laugh about . . .

Must tell Sharma and Baig about it and ask them what they think of artificial laughter, says Boota to himself.

Back home he goes over the scene again. He wonders, if artificial laughter can lighten people's minds then artificial crying must do some good as well. He has a close lady friend who is Shia. Once married to a Sunni, lived abroad for many years with him and her children; Westernized, sophisticated, erudite, knowing both Urdu and English; enjoys whisky and mild flirtation. But come Muharram, the first month of the Muslim calendar, a change comes over her. She often wears a black kurta, refuses to touch alcohol, has *majlis* (assembly) of Shias in her home where they recite *mersias* (elegies) in honour of Imam Hussain who was killed in the battle of Karbala many centuries ago. Many people break down in sobs and shed tears. Some beat their breasts in mourning. On the tenth day of Muharram (Ashura), the mourning reaches its crescendo, with Shias marching down public thoroughfares flogging themselves with nailed chains till they draw blood, and slapping their breasts crying, 'Ya Hassan, Ya Hussain.'

'Doesn't make sense to me,' said Boota to his lady friend after she had resumed taking an evening drink with him.

'Yes, it does,' she asserted firmly. 'Grieving and shedding tears cleanses one's system of meanness and pettiness.'

It still did not make sense to Boota. Dispute over the succession to the Caliphate split Muslims into two irreconcilable factions—Sunnis and Shias. They have separate mosques, rarely intermarry, abuse each other— a Shia is a *khatmal* (bedbug), a Sunni a *pissoo* (louse) or *machhar* (mosquito); Sunnis chant *madhey sahiba* (praises of the first three caliphs), Shias retaliate with *tabarriaah* (execrating them). They bomb each other's mosques. In short, they hate each other more than they hate infidels.

Must ask Baig about this, says Boota to himself.

That evening, as soon as they have greeted each other and enquired whether everything is hunky-dory, Boota tells them about his morning experiences.

'It is an ancient practice known as *hasya yoga*,' says the *sabjantawala*—know-all—Pandit Sharma. 'It is well known that laughter is the best medicine. It has the qualities of healing both mind and body. The Greeks also had a word for it—*gelos*—which means laughter, from which the English word gelotology—therapeutic laughter—is derived. Boota, I bet you don't know that word—when you get home look it up in your dictionary.'

Boota ignores Sharma's attempt at one-upmanship and asks, 'Is laughter healing even if it is artificial? Why not simply get someone to tickle your armpits?'

'No matter how you make yourself laugh, you must have a hearty laugh at least once a day,' replies Sharma.

'I don't understand what artificial laughing can do when there is nothing to laugh about,' says Baig. 'By all means laugh when you see something comical, hear a good joke,

when somebody makes a fool of himself; but ha-ha ha-ha
for nothing makes no sense to me.'

'What about people who never laugh?' asks Boota.
'That fellow who was Election Commissioner, what was
his name? Oh yes, Seshan. He never laughed; Mamata
Banerjee never laughs, Mehbooba Mufti never laughs.
Something wrong with them?'

'I have no idea,' replies Baig, 'but I feel uneasy in the
company of such people. Don't you agree, Sharmaji?'

'Fully,' replies Sharma. 'I have no such problem. I see
Boota every day—so have plenty to laugh about.'

'Me too,' says Baig. 'The evenings he is not there I feel
depressed. The Almighty in His wisdom created Sardars
to keep us laughing.'

Boota senses Sharma is trying to needle him; he is
always making fun of Sikhs, as most Hindus do. 'Sharma
Pandit,' he hits back, 'you make fun of Sardars all the
time. Let me tell you, only people who have confidence
in themselves can make fun of themselves. Here we are
today, a mere two per cent of the population, and we
are ruling the country: Sikh prime minister, Sikh head
of the Planning Commission, and until recently, Sikh
commander-in-chief.'

Sharma is amused. 'Baig Sahib, you know how hot-
headed these Sardars can be: they may laugh at themselves
but they cannot stand other people laughing at them. Ask

him why he gets so worked up when somebody asks him *"Baara baj gaye?"'*

'I don't get incensed,' protests Boota. 'Some years ago I was at a conference in Scotland. Among the invitees was the Bangladeshi poet Jasimuddin. Every morning at breakfast he would ask me in his Bengali-accented Hindi: *"Shordarji, aap ko boro boj gaya?"* And I would reply, *"Mera boro boj gaya."* Then he would explain: "It is beeg joke in my country." The poor fellow never caught on that I was mimicking his thick Bengali accent, so I was the one who had the last laugh.'

'Why has it got stuck on Sardarjis and no one else?' asks Baig.

'I'll tell you,' replies Boota. 'One version is when the Sikhs finally succeeded in blowing up the walls of Multan fort and capturing its rulers, the news reached Lahore a couple of days later at noontime. Maharaja Ranjit Singh was overjoyed and ordered cannons to be fired and gave his victorious soldiers the freedom to rape any woman they liked—which they did. That is why "baara bajey" rankles in the minds of non-Sikhs to this day.'

'Nonsense,' says Sharma angrily. 'I've taught Punjab history for some years; never heard of it. You have made it up.'

'But there must be something to it,' protests Baig. 'It could not have dropped from the air.'

'I can give you the answer,' says Boota. 'I stumbled on it by accident when I happened to be visiting Turkey. I was given two Turkish students to escort me. I asked them to tell me some Turkish jokes. Most of them were like ours, about foolish rulers, cuckolded husbands, mothers-in-law, etc. Then one of them told me that many of their jokes were about a peasant community called Laz living along the Caspian Sea. They are simple-minded peasants who lose their cool at noon. I am sure it must be Turkish soldiers in Muslim invaders' armies, maybe your ancestors, who brought the "baara bajey" joke and planted it on the Sikhs who are mostly simple-minded peasants.'

'Bootaji, *koi Sardarji joke ho jai*—some Sardar jokes please. *Chondee-chondee*, dripping with smut as you Punjabis say,' says Baig.

It is the opportunity Boota has been waiting for, to get even with Sharma. 'It is very non-vegetarian,' says Boota. 'Sharma won't like it.'

'Go ahead,' says Sharma, 'I won't mind.'

So Boota goes ahead. 'Once a Sardarji applied for a job. He was asked to come for an interview. There were three members of the interview board, all three Punjabi Hindus. They decided to make a chootia of the Sardar.

'As he sat down to face them, the first man said, "I will make a sound. You have to tell us what it is: *koo, chhuk chhuk, chhuk.*"

'"It is a railway train," answered the Sardar.

'"Quite right," said the board member. "What is it, Rajdhani or Shatabdi?"

'"Rajdhani."

'"Wrong. It is a Shatabdi."

'The second member asked him, "I will make a sound, you tell me what it is: bhow, wow, wow."

'"It is a dog barking."

'"Quite right. Is it a spaniel or an Alsatian?"

'"Alsatian."

'"Wrong. It is a spaniel."

'And so it went on till their questions were finished. Finally, the Sardarji turned to them and said, "You have asked me a lot of questions. Can I now ask you one?"

'"Yes, of course," they replied. "Go ahead."

'The Sardarji picked up a piece of paper from the table in front of him, drew a picture of the middle of a woman and asked, "Can you tell me what this is?"

'"Sure," they replied. "It is a *choot* or what you Sikhs call a *phuddee*."

'"Quite right," said the Sardarji, "now tell me, is it your mother's or your sister's?"'

Baig explodes into guffaws. Sharma remarks, 'Not very funny. I've heard it many times before from you.'

Baig continues to roar with laughter. Three hijras who periodically go round Lodhi Gardens to pester lovers cuddling behind bushes till they shell out money to be left alone, hear the loud laughter from the Boorha Binch. They recognize Baig because they have often sung and danced at his gates at weddings and births. They go to the bench and start clapping their hands and gyrating. Baig loses his cool. He pulls out a hundred-rupee note, hands it to the leading hijra and says firmly *'Dal fay ain ho jao—* Get lost. If you ever come here again I'll have you thrashed the next time you come to my house.' They bless him and go away.

Boota can't hold back. 'So Nawab Sahib, you also enjoy this diversion?'

'La haul billah Quwwat Allah Billah!' exclaims Baig. 'But if you want to add to your experiences, I'll send these fellows to your daulat khana. I'll pay their fee.'

They bid each other goodbye.

~

The discussion on the pros and cons of artificial mourning is taken up the next evening. Boota tells them about his Shia lady friend and what she had to say on the subject. Baig responds first. 'We are Sunnis, not Shias. We also mourn the martyrdom of Imam Hussain at Karbala but we do not beat our breasts or torture ourselves.'

'We have our martyrs too—all communities have a few. We honour them on their death anniversaries but do not make public demonstration of grief. Shias must be the only people who do so,' adds Sharma.

'That is not quite correct,' breaks in Boota. 'I recall in my village in Punjab whenever there was a death, groups of *mirasi* women would arrive on the scene and beat their breasts crying *hai-hai, hai-hai* along with chanting the name of the dead person. It was quite frightening, but that was customary. They had to be paid to go away.'

'That's not the same thing,' cuts in Sharma. 'Grief has to be spontaneous, not artificial. When anyone close to you dies, you break down and shed tears. If you don't, there is something wrong with you. These whites think that breaking down and crying is bad form. They bottle up their grief—cry when they are alone. Some wear black armbands or black ties for a few days. Even that practice has been given up. You take it from me, if you suppress sorrow and refuse to give expression to it, you have psychological problems. That is one reason why so many Westerners consult psychiatrists regularly. Don't you agree with me, Baig Sahib?'

'Shia Muslims are not the only ones nor the first to make mourning into a ritual,' interrupts Boota. 'Long before them the Jews had their Wailing Wall in Jerusalem, just below the Dome of the Rock and the Al Aqsa Mosque occupied by Israel. To this day it is a place of pilgrimage for them. They face the wall and cry their hearts out. Crying does lighten the heart.'

'Yes and no,' says Baig. 'Ghalib often mentions the *nauhagar*—a professional mourner. He says if he could afford it he would always have one with him. He also writes about the cleansing effect of weeping copious tears—you shed them and you feel washed clean and become *paak*—pure. Bootaji, I am sure you know these lines by heart.'

As one who never misses an opportunity to show off, Boota recites: '*Itney dhoye gaye ke bas paak ho gaye.* Okay, we are all agreed crying is as good for one as laughing,' says Boota. 'Now let us get back to our homes and cry heartily.'

∾

On the evening of the 14th of February, Sharma is in an unusually jovial mood, bursting to tell his friends news of great importance. No sooner than they greet each other and take their seats, he says, 'You know what?'

'What?' says Boota dutifully.

'I received four St Valentine cards today; four women declaring their love for me.'

'So did you make love to them?' asks Boota.

'I went to Khan Market and got four Valentine's Day cards. I tell you it was quite a problem. They keep them hidden in their drawers lest these goondas of the Shiv Sena and Bajrang Dal smash up their shops. They think it is against Indian culture and should be put down by force, if necessary. The fellow sold me the cards because he knows me. I sent them by courier to all the four ladies.'

'Please enlighten me about St Valentine. I have never heard of the gentleman,' says Baig.

Boota enlightens him and tells him of the practice of sending cards, which is prevalent in the West. 'What you are shy of putting in words, you do by post. Don't you read any English paper, Baig? Page after page full of messages of love in simple or code language. It is a multi-crore business. We Indians have a genius for picking up the worst habits of Westerners. Don't you agree, Sharmaji?'

Sharma feels uneasy as he is a great champion of India's traditional values. 'It is a harmless practice. Makes some people happy to know they are loved. It does less harm than writing names with drawings of hearts pierced by arrows on walls of ancient monuments and on tree trunks.'

'Both are asinine,' declares Boota. 'If you love somebody, go and tell him or her "I love you". They won't mind. Some may even respond. But this love by Speed Post or courier is beyond my comprehension.'

'This is not ishq, it is *ishtiharbaazi*—advertising,' says Baig. 'Love is something personal, strictly private, not to tell the world.'

'Ghalib writes about *namabars*—message carriers. But they only carried love letters because postal services were non-existent,' adds Baig. 'Anyway, Sharmaji, what did you do with the ladies to whom you sent these expensive greeting cards?'

'Nothing,' replies Sharma. 'You are not meant to do anything.'

'Then why do you object to the Shiv Sainiks or Bajrang Dalis preventing shopkeepers making money by selling meaningless cards?' asks Baig.

'Because it is none of their business. It is my money and I can spend it any way I like,' replies Sharma.

Boota interrupts their dialogue. 'For once I agree with Sharma. Those fundoos are Hindu Talibans; the Afghan Taliban force women to wear burqas, flog them if they wear jeans, stone them to death if they are caught making love to anyone besides their husbands. Ours rough up people, wreck their property. They don't object to sculptures in Konark or Khajuraho which depict couples copulating—they are ancient works of Hindu art—but if someone like Husain paints a Hindu goddess in the nude, they wreck his exhibitions, file criminal suits against him and force the poor chap, perhaps India's greatest living artist, to live in exile in Qatar. I say crush them now, or they will crush us later. I spit on their faces and spit on their bottoms.'

'Cool down, Sardar,' says Sharma. 'This is no way of celebrating St Valentine's Day. Go home and write a long love letter to someone willing to read it.'

So ends the 14th of February 2009 for members of the Sunset Club.

Half the month remains. Attendance at the Sunset Club becomes irregular. On the 15th, all three are there but the next day Boota is missing. 'What's happened to the Sardar?' asks Baig. 'No idea,' replies Sharma. 'I will send my servant across to find out.' Boota is missing again the next evening. Sharma tells Baig why: 'His elder brother died yesterday.'

'*Inna lillah-e-va inna Ilah-e-Rajaoon*,' intones Baig. 'That means what God gave you goes back to God. We Muslims recite this when we hear of a death. Was he ailing?'

'He was two or three years older than Boota. Was in a wheelchair for over five years. Was very hard of hearing. You could hardly understand what he was trying to say. Day and night the entire family of wife and four children were attending to him. What more can anyone ask for in one's last years on earth?'

'He must have been a good, God-fearing man,' proclaims Baig.

'Strange thing,' says Sharma. 'He was devoted to the one daughter he had. She was living in America—some kind of professor. When he started to sink, they sent word to her. It was mid-term but she took leave and flew back to be by her father's side. The strange thing is that she reached Delhi about 6 p.m., got home half an hour later, was holding his hand when he breathed his last. Almost as if he had been waiting for her before he departed forever.'

'I have heard other cases of the same kind—people holding on to life till they have seen the person they love most. God grants them their last wish,' says Baig.

Another two evenings pass without Boota. 'How many days of mourning are slated for the Sikhs?' asks Baig.

'They have the same as we Hindus,' replies Sharma. 'It can be *chautha*—fourth day—*shraadh* or *dahaya*—ten days—when they have an *antim ardas*—last prayer. But Boota never believed in rituals—or so he says. You never know about him.'

Boota takes his time and turns up four days later. Baig offers his condolences. He brushes them aside and says, 'He was as good as dead for the last five years. It was as much a relief for him as for his family. And now Amita Malik and Victor Kiernan have also died. All within a week.'

'Who was the *mohtarma*? Should I be knowing about her? And Kiernan Sahib?' asks Baig.

'What world do you live in?' demands Boota. 'Ask any educated Indian and he will tell you. Amita Malik was the best-known critic of radio and TV programmes. A Bengali Hindu married to a Punjabi Muslim. And Kiernan, the best translator of Urdu poetry, Faiz and Ghalib. A Scotsman who lived in Lahore for some years. His translations are available in all bookstores.'

'My apologies to both,' says Baig. 'I hardly listen to the radio or switch on TV. And I read Ghalib and Faiz in Urdu. Why do I need translations in English?'

'Quite right,' says Sharma. 'It's chaps like you, Boota, who know very little Urdu who read translations to show off your knowledge.'

Boota is not one to let Sharma get away with a jibe. 'O Panditji, I at least read the books I have. You only stock them as *deemak*—termite—feed.'

Baig has a hearty laugh. 'I don't have any English books. Deemak can't read Urdu, so they leave them alone.'

As they get up to leave for their homes, Baig says, '*Khuda ki kasam*—I swear by God—when you gentlemen don't come to the park, I get depressed and don't enjoy my dinner.'

Boota replies, 'Bhai Sahib, all of us are getting on in years. We have to prepare ourselves for the day the *mehfil* will be over.' And he quotes a Punjabi verse:

Not forever does the bulbul sing;
Not forever lasts the spring;
Not forever does happiness reign
Not forever do voices in majlis ring.

'Wah, wah,' applauds Baig. 'But we must keep meeting as long as we can. *Jab tak chaalee chaley.*' And adds Bahadur Shah Zafar's couplet:

I asked for a long life,
Only four days were granted:
Two went in hoping,
Two lost in waiting.

3

SPRING INTO SUMMER

In March, death and rebirth go hand in hand. It is the time of *patjhar* (falling leaves) and new ones taking their place. Peepals, neems, kosams and many others denude themselves to don new garments. Shahtoot (mulberry) trees, which looked like clothless umbrellas of dry sticks, get a green fuzz by mid-February; and by Holi, which fell this year on the 11th of March, they are laden with green or purple caterpillar-like fruit, much relished by Holi revellers. It is also the time of courtship among birds. Sparrows, rarely seen in Delhi now, used to be a sight to watch: the cock strutting around his lady friend who pretended to be indifferent to his amorous advances. Then changing her mind, squatting on her legs and exposing her cloaca to let him mount her. It is the same with other species of birds. They display their plumage, dance around their females till they get roused and allow themselves to be mounted. Seeds of new life are sown.

Somehow, a similar pattern of death–rebirth took place in human affairs. The Congress and its allies led by Manmohan Singh as prime minister ended their five-year tenure and general elections were announced. Needless to say it is the hot topic of discussion at the Sunset Club when it meets on the evening of the 2nd of March. Sharma opens the debate with a barb aimed at Boota.

'So Bootaji, the five-year rule of the Sardars comes to an end and we have to choose a new government.' Before Boota can reply, he adds: 'Mind you, I have nothing against Manmohan Singh. He was a good scholar, a topper in every exam, got a first at Cambridge. He was a good teacher. His ambition was to be professor of economics and settle down in Chandigarh. All that changed when he got a UN job with a fat dollar salary and moved to New York. And back as governor of the Reserve Bank of India. It was Prime Minister Narasimha Rao who made him finance minister and had him elected to the Rajya Sabha from Assam. On his own he would not have won a panchayat election. It is the same now. Sonia Gandhi knows Indians won't accept an Italian-born woman as prime minister, and her son Rahul is too young and inexperienced to be PM. So they put a harmless, unambitious man as their proxy. The real rulers of the country are Sonia and Rahul, not Manmohan Singh. Advani calls him *nikamma*—useless.'

'Oy, oy, oy, Pandit Sharma, what world do you live in?' retorts Boota. 'He is the best prime minister we have had so far: scholarly, highly experienced, he's turned around the economy of the country. Everyone is better off than he was five years ago. Remember, when he had his heart surgery a few months ago there were prayers offered in temples, mosques, churches, gurdwaras all over the country, just as they were when Amitabh Bachchan had his accident and was said to be dying. We will soon see whether the people of this country think *he* is nikamma or that Sindhi hero of Hindu fundoos. What do you have to say, Baig?'

'Bhai, I don't involve myself in politics,' Baig replies. 'I go along with my Begum: she says Manmohan is a *bhalamanas, sharif* and *mita hua*—a good man, a gentleman and self-effacing. What more can you ask of a prime minister?'

That is not good enough for Boota. He challenges Sharma. 'Panditji, will you take a bet with me on who will be the next PM—Advani or Manmohan?'

Sharma shrugs him off. 'I don't make foolish bets. And frankly I don't care who wins, it's six of one, half a dozen of the other. In any case I won't be voting. My servants do and all they tell me later is "we voted for the Hindu party".'

'That means BJP, doesn't it?' asks Baig. 'I too don't vote; too old to stand in a line for an hour or more. But my Begum, servants and their wives vote for the *panja*—the hand, the symbol of the Congress Party—as they have done in every election.'

Sharma ends the debate with words of advice. 'It is best to wait till the time to decide is near. Weigh the pros and cons of the contesting parties, their past performance and the promises they make. At every election, *ghareebee hatao*—banish poverty—they say. But poverty is very much there. They promise *roti, kapra* and *makaan*—food, clothing and a roof over their heads. After sixty-two years, half the population goes hungry, all the kapra it has is a *langoti* and most people live in mud huts or hovels. And corruption is rampant. We are counted among the most corrupt nations of the world. We make big claims when we should be hanging our heads in shame.'

Sharma is impressed by his own words. As usual Boota punctures his ego. 'I have a bright idea to solve all our country's problems. Let us ignore Advani and Manmohan Singh and elect Pandit Sharma as the prime minister of India. What do you say, Baig?'

'Hundred per cent okay if Sharmaji is willing.'

Sharma maintains a dignified silence before delivering the punchline. 'It is no use wasting one's breath on people like you. You think elections are just a tamasha enacted every five years. Good night.'

They get up from the Boorha Binch to return to their homes.

After the end of the first week, attendance at the Sunset Club becomes somewhat erratic. On the 9th evening Baig announces, 'Bhai, I will not be able to come tomorrow evening.'

'*Khair to hai*—all is well?' asks Sharma.

'*Allah ka shukar hai*—God be thanked,' replies Baig, raising both hands. 'Tomorrow is Eid-e-Milad-un-Nabi. Our holy Prophet died on his birthday; that is why we also call it Bara Wafaat.'

'So do you celebrate his birthday or mourn his death?' asks Sharma.

'We do both. It symbolizes the oneness of births and deaths—where there is birth, death is bound to be, they go hand in hand. My Begum insists I stay at home all day to receive callers who come to exchange Eid greetings; I go to the mosque for afternoon prayers and to the Nizamuddin Dargah to make offerings for the *langar*—community kitchen. It is *zakaat*—charity—which is obligatory in Islam.'

Boota needles him, 'What I know about Mussalmans celebrating is they get into new clothes, hug each other three times, offer namaaz on the roads and eat a lot of dates and vermicelli pudding. Am I right, Baig Sahib?'

'More or less,' replies Baig, 'but unlike you Hindus and Sikhs we do not take out huge processions with bands, elephants, gatka players, singers, etc., which bring city life to a standstill. Shops have to close down, daily wagers earn nothing. People miss their flights and trains; the sick can't get to hospitals in time. You are welcome to your celebrations at other people's inconvenience.'

'Touché,' says Sharma, using one of the eight words of French he remembers. He explains: 'In fencing—you know fencing? Mock fight with blunted rapiers, when one man hits the other, he scores a point and the referee shouts "touché" and grants him victory. I say touché in favour of Baig. He scored over us.' And after a short pause he adds, 'Incidentally, I will not be coming day after tomorrow; it is Holi and I expect my friends and relatives will drop in to greet me.'

'Not Holi, but *hullarbaazi*, rowdyism. Throw coloured water on people, rub red powder on girls' cheeks and feel their breasts, gamble and drink bhang,' remarks Boota. 'What is religious about it?'

Sharma retorts, 'You only see the ugly side of everything. Take some good bhang in a glass of warm, sweetened milk and you will sleep like a log for twenty-four hours.'

The three have a hearty laugh. 'We will resume our sessions after the festivals,' says Baig as they part company.

◦

On Holi evening Sharma is missing from the Boorha Binch. 'He must be enjoying his *bara* peg of bhang,' says Boota to Baig.

'Have you ever tasted it?' asks Baig.

'Occasionally,' replies Boota. 'It is like taking several sleeping tablets. Sound sleep. No hangover. Nihangs are addicted to it. They make a concoction of almonds, milk and bhang and call it *sukkha parshad*—the peace giver. They are big braggarts who do no work—*nikhattoos*.'

'Sounds like opium, it has the same effect. A little taken occasionally does no harm. If one becomes an *afeemchee*, an addict, then one becomes useless. I say moderation in everything, be it alcohol or drugs. Preachers of prohibition make too much noise.'

'They can go bugger themselves,' says Boota with an air of finality.

They fall silent for a few moments till Boota comes out with something that has been on his mind for a long time. 'Baig, we—Sharma and I—have told you everything about ourselves, but you keep everything to yourself.'

'What do you mean! What do you want to know about me?'

'Your sex life. It can't have been limited to your Begum.'

'So you can tell the world about it with the beat of a drum?'

'No, no,' assures Boota, 'I won't even tell Sharma. Khuda ki kasam.'

'I will tell you, but if a word leaks out, I'll have nothing more to do with you. What do you want to know?'

'The most memorable sex encounter you have had in your life.'

Baig looks around to make sure no one is close by. 'It was many years ago; Begum Sakina had gone to her parents as she was expecting a child. I was anxious to get some distraction. I had heard of a courtesan who called herself Noor Mahal. She had retired from her profession but had found very beautiful girls from royal families, who had fallen on hard times. She had trained them to dance and sing at her set-up in Chawri Bazaar, behind the Jama Masjid. I decided to go there. I told my chauffeur to drop me in the open square behind the Royal Mosque and wait for me. I walked to the *kotha* and went up the stairs. I was welcomed by the Madame. She recognized me as a fellow Muslim. When I mentioned my name, she guessed who I was and was gushing in her welcome. "We are honoured, our kismet has woken up," and that sort of thing. There were three men before me—all rich. The mujra was on. We exchanged salaams and I sat down on the carpet and reclined on bolsters. The Madame asked me if I would like a whisky, and whether I had any *farmaish*—request—for a song. I replied, "Let them sing what they like best."

'It was after I had had a few pegs of whisky that I had a good look at the dancing girls. All of them were good looking but one stood out. She was tall as a cypress, slender, with almond-shaped eyes, full-bosomed, with a slim waist and beautifully rounded buttocks. Her black hair fell to her waist. I swear she looked like a houri come down from Paradise. I could not keep my eyes off her. She noticed the adoration in my eyes and gave me a winsome smile. I sat through two mujra performances, threw hundred-rupee notes at the girls and the sarangi and tabla players. I'd had three whiskies when the Madame came and whispered in my ear: "Nawab Sahib, would you like any of the girls for a more intimate relationship?"

'I whispered back, "The tall one, if she is willing."

'She took me by the hand and led me to a room at the back. It had large mirrors, a double bed and vases full of roses. A minute later the girl came in and bowed an *aadaab* to me. The Madame introduced her as Mastaani. I am sure that was not her real name but a professional pseudonym. The Madame left us and shut the door behind us. Mastaani put up the latch and took off the bells from her ankles. She spoke to me, "Nawab Sahib, how did your benign eyes fall on this humble maidservant?"

'"*Mashallah*—Allah be praised. He has bestowed you with such beauty. I could not take my eyes off you. How did you land in a place like this? You should be living in a palace."

'She slapped her forehead with her palm and replied, "My fate. If Allah wills, I may find a rich husband and become a respected Begum."

'She blushed a deep red. She took off her shirt, threw it on the carpet and covered her eyes with both hands. "That is not enough," I said, pulling her closer to me. With a quick movement I pulled the cord of her salwar. It fell around her feet. She had shaved off her pubic hair— I find pubic hair very off-putting—she was like a white marble statue without a blemish on her body.

'I laid her beside me on the bed. Then I began to kiss her from her eyes, cheeks, neck, bosom, belly, pubis, thighs, legs, down to her feet and back to her forehead. She stretched her hand and undid my trouser belt and felt my penis. "Lord, help me!" she exclaimed. "It's huge— the biggest I have ever seen! It will rip me apart. Be gentle with me."

'I was flattered—all men are flattered when a woman praises the size of their tool. So I was very gentle when I put it in her. She gripped it firmly with her inner muscles and began to milk it as if it were a cow's udder. I told her to stop because I did not want it to come to an end so quickly. I stayed in her till she had two orgasms and cried out in ecstasy. And a third one when I began to thrust in with great vigour and poured my seed into her. Bootaji, I have never enjoyed sex as I did that evening.'

'Then what happened?' asked Boota.

'I gave her three thousand rupees. She protested that it was too much but accepted it.'

'Did you go to her again?' asked Boota.

'I went three or four evenings. She said she had fallen in love with me and wanted me to marry her and keep her as one of my maidservants. That made me cool off her. The last time I went to her she told me she was pregnant by me. A prostitute who sleeps with a dozen men every week cannot impute paternity to any one of them. I never went back to her. That was the end of my affair with Mastaani. It keeps coming back to me and I always wanted to tell somebody about it. So I told you, Boota Singh. Now you honour your word and never spill it out to another soul. Or I will murder you.'

'Never,' said Boota.

The sun had almost set, the park was almost empty. They bade farewell to each other.

❦

Baig, who is normally cool about events in the country, is very worked up on the evening of the 19th of March. He is the first to take his seat on the Boorha Binch and is impatiently tapping his shoes with his walking stick, waiting for his friends to arrive. As soon as the other two join him and have greeted each other, Baig opens up: 'Hope you have read about the speech made by Maneka Gandhi's *launda* Varun in his election campaign in Pilibhit?

My Begum read it out to me. He said Muslims have frightful names like Fazlullah and other Ullahs and he will chop off our hands. That includes me because I am Barkatullah Baig.'

'Ghalib was also an Ullah—Asadullah Khan Ghalib,' adds Boota. 'And so is that fat woman from Bombay who claims to be a niece of Maulana Azad and was caught peddling a false photograph of herself with her uncle. She was a member of the Congress Party and now the BJP. She is Heptullah. You know how she explained her conversion? She said, "In everyone's life there comes a turn—*morh aata hai*," so she took a U-turn. From being a devotee of Mahatma Gandhi and worshipper of Indira Gandhi, when she discovered she had nothing more to gain from them, she turned to Veer Savarkar and L.K. Advani. No one trusts her.'

'I am sure Varun did not mean it that way,' says Sharma gently. 'His mother says the speech recorded was doctored.'

'What else would any mother say when her child makes an ass of himself?' asks Boota.

Baig is not appeased. 'It is shameful—*sharamnaak*. He says he does not want Muslims to vote for him. I am sure his party leaders would like to have Muslim votes. And yet none of them have condemned him. You will see, BJP will not get a single Muslim vote in the next general elections.'

Sharma again strikes a discordant note. 'It has a few Muslims holding important positions. One is the party secretary, another an elected MP and the fat lady you referred to is now an important leader of the BJP!'

'Turncoats are a dime a dozen,' says Boota. 'I can make a guess: if the Muslims lay their hands on Varun, they will not chop off his arms, but something more vital.'

That creates some laughter. Baig senses Boota is on his side and Sharma as non-committal as he always is.

On the 23rd of March the headline news in all papers is Ratan Tata's announcement that his company is to market a new car named Nano which will cost a mere one lakh rupees. Naturally it is the topic of debate among the members of the Sunset Club. As usual, Boota begins on an aggressive note. 'As it is, our roads are clogged with cars at all hours and now this Tata fellow is going to add to the chaos by introducing yet another brand. Every *lalloo-panjoo*—riff-raff—who rides a bicycle or a scooter will get a Nano and bring traffic to a standstill.'

Sharma protests: 'We should be proud of producing the cheapest car in the world—cheaper than anything China has produced. And you can take it from me that anything produced by a Parsi is top-class quality. It is the job of the municipalities and state governments to widen roads and build flyovers. Don't you agree, Baig Sahib?'

Baig laughs and replies, 'I entirely agree with both of you. Five years ago it used to take me five to seven minutes to get from Nizamuddin to Lodhi Gardens. Now it takes me fifteen minutes to half an hour, because the short stretch of Mathura Road is always jammed with cars. However, I have put my name on the list of applicants for a Nano. My Begum wanted me to do so. My Mercedes cost me over fifty lakh rupees; my Maruti Swift over five lakh. By comparison the price of the Nano is nothing. And Boota Singhji, I am not a lalloo-panjoo. I am Nawab Barkatullah Baig Dehlavi.'

'May your Nano prove a blessing—mubarak,' sneers Boota. 'Why not get ten, one for each servant? You can then call yourself Nawab Nano Wala of Nizamuddin?'

'*Inshallah*, may your tongue be coated with honey,' says Baig, ending the debate.

On the morning of the 25th of March there is a mild drizzle. It washes away the dust and makes trees and lawns look cleaner and greener. It also brings down the temperature by a degree or two and raises hopes that spring has not succumbed to summer's heat. Members of the Sunset Club are in high spirits when they meet in the evening. 'What a blessing a few drops of rain can be,' says Baig. '*Yeh khushbahar mausam*, I hope, will last a few more days.'

'Seasons do not change to please humans,' says Sharma. 'They are ordained by the inscrutable laws of nature.'

'Whatever that means,' cuts in Boota, 'only Panditji knows; he has a hotline communication with nature.'

Sharma lets the sarcasm pass. Baig changes the topic. 'You recite a poem in praise of spring, Bootaji.'

Boota rustles his memory. 'There is Mir Taqi Mir's spring song. You know he lived in Delhi while Abdali ransacked the city. Ghalib acknowledges him as the master of Urdu poetry.'

'So let's have it,' requests Baig.

Boota goes over the lines in his mind before he recites:

If you like to visit a garden, go
Now, for this is the month of Spring;
The leaves are green and flowering trees
Are in full bloom. The clouds hang low,
And gentle rain is falling.
The heart feels like a throbbing wound,
The tears have turned to one red flood;
This crimson-faced poppy of love
Dries up life and drains all blood

This is the time when fresh, green leaves
Appear upon the trees;
And branch and twig of plant and shrub
Are bent with bloom and seed.

With blaze of roses' colour, Mir,
The garden is on fire;
The bulbul sounds a warning note:
'Go past, O sir, beware.'

'Wah, wah!' Baig and Sharma applaud.

4

NOW THAT APRIL
IS HERE

Sharma is in his armchair in the sitting room, munching
cornflakes mixed with warm milk and honey, a mug
of tea sits on the side table. Dabboo Three sleeps near his
feet, and the servants' children watch TV before they
leave for school; it is Wednesday. Sharma finishes his
cornflakes-with-honey breakfast, takes out his dentures
before he has tea. The dentures are put in a bowl of water
in the bathroom. Sharma's face minus his dentures looks
somewhat squashed. He takes a sip of the tea. Dabboo
Three turns his head enquiringly towards his master as if
to indicate: 'I hear footsteps outside our flat, let's find

out.' He howls and barks. Pavan follows him and picks up a letter and hands it to his master. Sharma takes a look at the envelope; it has no stamp and has been delivered by hand. He examines the handwriting; he is not familiar with it. The way he is addressed pleases him: To, The Hon'ble Shri Preetam Sharma, Scholar Emeritus of Wisdom, New Delhi.

He tears open the envelope; it has no letterhead giving name, address or telephone number of the writer. Nor a date. The handwriting is bold and calligraphic. It reads:

Dear Beloved Professor Sahib, you don't know me but I know you very well. I am a college teacher, fifty years old. I have attended all your lectures wherever they were delivered. I cherish every word you said but did not have the courage to speak to you. All I want from you is permission to sit at your feet, press your legs and be close to you. I am not asking for too much, am I? If you are willing to accept me, please put a single rose in a vase by the window which can be seen from the outside and I will know the answer is yes. Then I will come over and disclose my identity. Or I will not bother you and admire you from a distance. With love and adoration, your great admirer.

Sharma is perplexed. He reads the letter a second, then a third time. He recalls some of the lectures he had delivered. There were two or three women who were always present. He cannot recall what they looked like. It could be one of them. Or was it a hoax? He is pleasantly puzzled.

On his way back after lunch at the India International Centre, Sharma stops at the florist shop in Khan Market. 'Give me a rose, the best you have,' he says.

'Just one, sahib? No one buys a single flower. Take at least four or six to put in your vase. They'll look nice and you can enjoy their scent.'

'Today I'll take only one,' replies Sharma. 'How much?'

'Five rupees,' replies the florist as he hands him a dark purple rose with a long stem. Then he turns to his boy assistants and mutters, '*Kameena*—miser. Only one flower.'

Sharma is back home. Before he retires for his siesta, he asks Pavan to put the rose in a tumbler of water—he has no narrow vase for a single flower—and place it by the window. During his afternoon siesta he dreams about the possible outcome.

One evening while doing a round of Lodhi Gardens, Boota noticed a few flame of the forest trees in bloom near Muhammad Shah Sayyid's tomb. And three corals in flower behind Sheesh Gumbad. Both have a very short span of blossoming—hardly a week or ten days. So Boota decides to take a drive along the Ridge where they grow in profusion.

Having had his morning mug of tea, he drives to the Ridge. At that early hour there is very little traffic—some morning walkers, *doodhwalas* with cans of buffalo milk dangling from the bars of their cycles, and paperwalas distributing daily newspapers in different localities. The Ridge is deserted but on either side he can see flames and corals in flower. He can now tell his friends and impress them about being a nature lover. On his way back he goes past the roundabout on Sansad Marg facing Parliament, to see if the jacarandas are in flower. There is a cluster of them on the roundabout, which turn lavender blue when they are in full bloom. No flowers yet. Since there is hardly any traffic on the usually busy Sansad Marg, he drives to Connaught Circus which has a lot of gulmohars in its Central Park. Shops are closed. Only some morning walkers. He drives back to his home, pleased with having done his duty by nature. As he opens the door, he sees a letter lying on the floor. He examines the handwriting. He cannot recognize it. The honorific is designed to flatter him: 'The Right Hon'ble & Most Respected Sardar Boota Singh Ji, World Famous Writer, New Delhi.'

It brings a smile to his lips. He wishes it was true. He settles down in his armchair. Bahadur brings his tray with a glass of warm milk, carton of Isabgol and a bowl of sugar. He mixes his dosage of bowel-cleaner and tears open the envelope. It reads: 'Most respected Sardar Sahib, you don't know me. I am a humble teacher in a girls' college. But I have read every word you write in your weekly column. I preserve them as a sacred treasure. You write so beautifully, your ideas are so fresh and thought-provoking. You should have been awarded the Nobel Prize for Literature.'

Boota is flattered. He agrees with everything the lady teacher has written but he has not even been shortlisted for the Booker or the Pulitzer, nor even the Gnanpith or Sahitya Akademi awards.

He continues to read: 'It is my life's ambition to be close to you and be your *chelee*. I ask for nothing more. If you are willing to consider me as a pupil, just put a single rose flower in a vase and put it alongside your window so that it can be seen from the outside. If it is there I will knock at your door. If not, I will pray to God to grant you a long life to enlighten the human race.'

The letter is unsigned.

Boota muses over it for a long time. Was somebody pulling his leg? How did he or she read his mind? Whatever it was, there was no harm in giving it a try.

After his breakfast Boota walks over to the florist in Khan Market and asks for a single rose. 'What's happened to rose-lovers today?' wonders the florist. 'Nobody buys one flower—take at least six, it is *boni*—my first sale of the day.' Boota agrees to buy six and pays thirty rupees for them. Back home he puts five in one vase on the dining table and places the remaining one in another vase by the window.

There is no response the next day. The following day both Boota and Sharma find a note slipped under their front door. It has only one word inscribed on it in bold letters: 'Chootia'.

It then occurs to Boota that the day he got the first letter was Wednesday, the 1st of April—All Fools Day.

In the evening Sharma and Boota arrive at the Boorha Binch before Baig. Boota asks Sharma if he had received a love letter on the 1st of April. 'Yes,' replies Sharma. 'I took no notice of it. Very childish to play such pranks on old people. What did you do?'

'Nothing,' replies Boota. 'I saw through the game.'

Baig joins them. They tell him about the mysterious letters they received and the footnote that followed. Baig guffaws with laughter and says, 'It was one of the viceroys of India, I think it was Lord Curzon, who said there are three kinds of fools: ordinary fools, damn fools and bloody fools. You can choose which category you belong to. Since you made fools of yourselves only one day of the year you are damn or bloody fools. Don't mind my saying so!'

❧

Boota looks forward to evenings at home when his son is on his annual visit to Delhi, ostensibly 'to look after my old man while my sister is away'. But he hardly has time to talk to his old man. He spends his afternoons playing golf, and evenings catching up with his pals. He is rarely back before 2 a.m., and gets up around 10 a.m. Once in a while he joins his father at lunch, when they exchange a few words. And once in a while Boota realizes his son is back earlier than usual, as in his half-sleep he can hear voices coming from the TV set.

It was one of those rare evenings: his son was at home, sipping a mixture of lime juice and vodka from his large tankard. Some kind of cricket match was on TV and he was glued to it. Boota poured out a large single malt for himself in his crystal cut-glass tumbler, added soda and three cubes of ice and relaxed in his armchair. He could see the cricket in which he had no interest, and because of his growing deafness was not disturbed by the commentary. He sipped his Scotch, munched some wasabi peas and caviar on biscuits. He felt elevated and a little drowsy.

Exactly at 8 p.m. he signalled to Bahadur, 'Khana.' His son said to Bahadur, 'For me, later.' So Boota ate his solitary meal of prawns cooked in mustard in Bengali style, followed by a slice of chocolate cake. As usual, after the meal he asked himself, 'Did I eat too much?' And answered, 'I should not have taken all those canapés and cake.' He begins to nod with sleepiness. With great effort he gets up from his chair and without bidding his son goodnight makes his way to the bathroom, gargles and goes to his bedroom. He swallows ten pills, puts eye drops in his eyes, takes some chooran and reads a few couplets of Ghalib; he has read them a hundred times before. Then he switches off the bedside light. He is not sure whether he is in a stupor or really asleep. But he is transported to the land of dreams.

It is a rude awakening. He has fallen off his bed and is lying on the hard, cold cement floor. He has bruised a side of his forehead, shoulder, elbow and one knee. He feels his limbs to check whether he has broken a bone. Bones, though they appear hard, become brittle with age and snap easily. With old people they can seldom be rejoined. And if it is the pelvic bone, they can be sure of spending the rest of their days in a wheelchair before coming to an agonizing end. Having made sure he has not broken a bone, he crawls along the floor past his bed to clutch something to help him get up on his feet. It's no use. He can hear the TV and shouts for his son to come to his aid. His son can't get him up and calls a security guard to help him. The two haul him up. He thanks them and says, 'I am okay. I'll get back to bed. What time is it now?'

His son looks at his watch and replies: '12.30 a.m. Shall I send for the doctor?'

'No,' replies Boota and repeats: 'I am okay. I'll go to bed.'

He tries but sleep eludes him. He gives up and in the bedroom relaxes in his armchair and shuts his eyes. He broods. It was a narrow escape. If he had broken a bone, or worse, fractured his skull, it would have been the end. Does the mind perish with the body? If not, where does it go? Nowhere. He recalls faces of friends, mainly women he was close to. As their faces flash in his mind's screen, he asks, 'Honey, where are you? Celia, where are you? Elinor, where are you?' And so on. They give him winsome smiles but no one answers his question. Even they do not know where they are. No one has ever known what happens to a person when he dies. All this talk of rebirth, Day of Judgement, heaven or hell, are mere figments of man's imagination. Myths never die; they are passed on by one generation to the next. Myths are eternal. Having talked to himself for an hour or two, sleep overtakes him and he dozes off in his armchair. He is woken up by Bahadur bringing his morning mug of tea around 5 a.m.

At 7 a.m., Dr Malhotra, who has a clinic across the road in Khan Market, arrives to examine him. He has been summoned by his son who did not consult his father before doing so. Doctor Sahib opens his bag, takes out his stethoscope, his BP measuring machine, and gadgets to take a blood sample. Boota protests, 'Doctor Sahib, I only fell off my bed. I don't need all these tests.' Dr Malhotra ignores his remark and proceeds to check his chest and back, makes him take long breaths as he moves his stethoscope to different points of his chest and back. Then he takes his BP and pronounces, '130 by 80. Okay.' He pricks his forefinger and takes blood and pronounces, '250. A bit on the higher side. What happened?'

'Nothing,' replies Boota. 'I fell off my bed at midnight.'

'I see,' replies the doctor and makes him wave his arms and legs before pronouncing, 'No bones broken.'

He has a look at Boota's bed and pronounces the prescription to Boota's son. 'Put the bed next to the bookshelves so that there is no space to fall in. And two chairs on the other side so that he cannot fall on that side either.' He puts his gadgets back in his bag and tells his son: 'Rs 1,500. My fee for outside calls is Rs 1,500.'

Boota's son pays him cash and sees him off to the door.

'That was wholly unnecessary,' growls Boota. 'Any ass could have told you to put my bed against the wall on one side and chairs on the other to prevent my falling off. Waste of money.'

'I can afford it,' asserts his son. 'One must not take chances of accidents at your age.'

ॐ

Friday, the 3rd of April is Ram Navami, the birth anniversary of Shri Ram. We know the day of his birth but not the year he was born. It is generally accepted that he was born in Ayodhya and was the son of King Dashratha and Queen Kaushalya. All Hindus look upon him as God incarnate and his wife Sita as the Mother Goddess, the paragon of chastity and fidelity. Ram's younger brother, Lakshman is the prime example of a devoted younger sibling; and Hanuman the half-ape half-human is revered as a great warrior and caretaker of the divine family. To this day, people greet each other saying *Shri Ramji ki jai*, *Jai Shri Ram* or *Ram-Ram*. Anything left to fate is '*Ram bharosey*', and when a dead person is taken for cremation, the leading group shouts *Ram Naam Sat Hai*—the name of Ram is the truth; others respond *Sat Bolo Gat Hai*—speak the truth and find salvation.

Pandit Sharma and his sister are Ram Bhakts—worshippers of Shri Ram. The first thing Sharma's sister does in the morning is to put a red tilak on her forehead. On Ram Navami, they go to the Birla Mandir to pray. On the way back Sunita buys burfi and laddoos to offer to people who call on them bringing different kinds of sweets. That day, Sharma has to deliver many lectures on Hinduism to gatherings of learned people. He tells them that Hinduism is the oldest religion in the world. He tells them Hinduism is the only religion in the world which was not founded by a prophet but evolved entirely in the quest for the Eternal Truth. He tells them that Sanskrit is the mother of all the languages of the world. He tells them Hinduism is the most tolerant religion in the world, because it believes in the principle of live and let live. And so on and so forth. His audiences are enthralled by his discourses. Many of them come and touch his feet when he finishes his lectures.

Around Ram Navami, Sharma's presence at the Sunset Club becomes somewhat erratic, and it's only the other two members who find themselves on the Boorha Binch. Oddly enough, though they like and respect Sharma, they are more at ease when he is not there. Boota's language becomes more bawdy and Baig begs him to recount some of his salacious adventures in foreign lands. Boota opens up and recounts them with great relish. It was on Baig's farmaish that Boota came out with the story of his affair with an English lady professor in London.

'I don't remember who it was who took me to a party to celebrate the publication of a doctoral thesis on some aspect of sociology by a young lady lecturer. She had thrown an open-house party at which the invitees could bring their friends. There were nearly fifty men and women, mostly academics. They were served only red wine and cheese. I filled my wine glass and sat in a corner watching the scene. Our hostess, named Betty something, who was in her mid-twenties, looked more like a schoolboy than a grown-up woman. Her hair was cropped and barely covered her ears. She wore glasses. Her front teeth protruded out of her mouth. She appeared to be a chain smoker. She wore a brown sweater, covering her torso from neck to waist. She was very animated and had something to say to all her guests. She came and sat by me. "Who are you?" I told her who I was, what I was doing. She didn't seem interested. She asked, "Do you do yoga?" I replied, "I find it very boring." "You could not be more wrong," she asserted. "It is the best form of exercise in the world. Half an hour of different asanas in the morning, half an hour in the evening, exercise both mind and body; you feel on top of the world. Give it a try and see the difference it makes. You don't need to buy a book. I'll give you a few lessons for free. You can buy me dinner."

'I gave her my card. She looked at it. "Good, I am not far away. The other end of King's Road. Lots of good pubs and eateries on King's Road. I don't have a card. I'll write my phone number on your card. I am usually back from college by five in the evening. Ring me up whenever you are free."

'I did not want to show my eagerness to accept her offer, so I did not ring her up for the next two days. But I thought about her all the time, and my desire to know her better became compulsive. I rang her up the third evening and invited her over to my basement flat. She accepted readily and said, "I'll give you your first yoga lesson. You can give me dinner." I hurried out of my flat and got a couple of bottles of vintage Bordeaux, tidied up my sitting room and waited for her.

'As promised, she arrived punctually at 6.30 p.m. She was wearing a light grey blouse and long black skirt. She gave me a peck on my cheek and surveyed the room. "Not bad," she said, "and you too live all by yourself."

'"Yep. I like living alone. Make my own toast and coffee in the morning. Open a tin of tomato soup for lunch. Gourmet dinner. And back home before 9.30 p.m. Now, can I serve you some good wine?"

'"Not just now," she replied, "first a few yoga lessons."

'"Okay! Go ahead."

'She sat down on the carpet and did padma asan with deep breathing. Then dhanur asan, arching her neck and looking at the roof. I noticed she had a small bosom, her nipples stuck out of her blouse. "Get it?" she asked.

'"I can't bend my knees for the lotus pose. And I don't think it is of any consequence. I tried to stand on my head—our Prime Minister Nehru did that every day. I nearly broke my neck," I replied.

'"It is easy and very beneficial," she said. "Let me show you." She rested her head on her palms and slowly raised her legs skywards. Her skirt fell down on her face, baring her from waist to toe. She had a sanitary towel on under her panties. "My periods," she explained from

beneath the folds of her skirt. "Another couple of days.
Bloody nuisance."

'She lowered her torso, took a few long breaths and
said, "I am ready for the wine." She took out a cigarette
and said, "I may smoke another cigarette before we set
out. Some people don't smoke but drink like fish." We sat
and sipped our wine. I asked her where she was teaching.
She asked me what I did for a living. An hour passed. The
bottle of Bordeaux was finished.

'"Where shall we go for dinner?" I asked.

'"Round the corner. A good pub called The World's
End—bar on the ground floor, restaurant on the first floor."

'She took my arm as we walked to The World's End. The
bar was crowded. The barmen knew her and exchanged
greetings with her. We went up the stairs to the restaurant
and took a table by the window overlooking King's Road.
The waitress came with the menu. She also seemed to
know Betty. "Madam, what would you like this evening?"
Betty took a cursory look at the menu and replied, "I
leave it to you, give us what you think is best. First, a
bottle of Bordeaux."

'She lit a cigarette, blew smoke out of her nostrils and
reclined in her chair. "I feel good," she said. The waitress
uncorked the bottle, poured a little in my glass for
approval. I took a sip, rolled it round my mouth and said,
"Excellent." She filled our wine glasses and left the bottle
on our table.

'"I too feel good," I said. "You are good company."

'"Thanks, we must see more of each other," she said.

'"You are the busy one; I'll be available whenever it suits you."

'She got out her pocket diary and made sure she had my telephone number. "Okay, the ball is in my court," she said.

'The waitress brought our dinner. Steak, potatoes, garlic bread. "Bon appétit," she said, and left. I was hungry and the wine had whipped up my appetite.'

Baig interrupts, 'You mean you ate cow's meat? Isn't it forbidden for Sikhs?'

'It is,' replies Boota. 'I enjoy doing what is forbidden. I bet you have never tasted pork or ham or bacon. They can be very tasty. Try them if you have the guts to do so.'

'*Tauba, tauba!*' says Baig holding his ears. 'They are haram to a Muslim. Anyhow, get on with your Betty. Then what happened after the dinner?'

'Nothing much, except that when we parted she kissed me on the lips and said in French, *"A bientot"*, which means see you soon. It's odd, but I stayed at home waiting for her call. She did call three days later and asked me if I was free. "I'll bring packed dinner—Mexican—so we don't have to go out. You get some wine. Okay?" I said, "Okay." I got two bottles of Italian wine—a Chianti and a Barolo. And waited for her.

'She arrived at 6.30 p.m., carrying a large carton of food and a rucksack on her back. I greeted her warmly with a prolonged kiss on her lips. She placed the things on the floor and told me to put the carton in the kitchen. "It will need heating up. Meanwhile yoga, and then we can have some wine."

'She went through the usual asanas, and once again her skirt fell down and covered her face. But this time she wore no underwear. From the tips of her toes down to her waist including her cunt and belly button, she was exposed to me. I got the message. She got back on her feet and sat next to me. Her hand rested on my middle. She felt my erection and said to me, "I see you liked what you saw." And without further ado divested herself of all her clothes. We made love on my sofa. After we finished, she did not put on her clothes but sat stark naked, smoking and sipping wine. "You warm the dinner while I take a shower." She went to the bathroom, leaving her clothes on the sofa. She took a shower and came back. She sat down on the sofa, lit another cigarette and sipped more wine.

'Before we ate our dinner, we had a second round of lovemaking. This time I lasted much longer, and she shivered and moaned as she climaxed. We had the Mexican dinner she had brought. She stayed naked. We finished the second bottle of wine. We were both somewhat drunk and tired. She lay alongside me on the sofa for a long time till we were heavy with sleep. Without clearing the table I led her to my bedroom and, like her, divested myself of all my clothes. She slept naked in my arms. Early next morning we made love again and she had yet another orgasm. I gave her coffee and buttered toast for breakfast. She left for her college, promising to return in the evening.

'It became a routine. I had a month left before I returned to India. All that month she stayed with me. We drank wine and made love every day. She liked to stay naked. She said clothes are for going out, at home one should stay naked. Her naked, boyish figure haunts me to this day.

'Baig, imagine a stark naked girl around you all day, all night. And upside down twice a day. I tell you, Baig, neither long, curly jet-black hair, nor almond eyes or scarlet lips, not even the hairy cunt which is his main target, can excite a man's lust as much as buttocks seen from the rear, beautifully rounded and dimpled.' Boota cups the palms of his hand and outlines fulsome curves to demonstrate what he means. 'They make an impotent man get an erection. And I was not impotent at that time. She drained every ounce of semen I had in my body.'

'Did you keep in touch with her?' asks Baig.

'For some time. Then she got married to some professor and had a couple of children. Then the marriage broke

up. I heard from a mutual friend that she gave up teaching
and writing books, to become a full-time yoga teacher. I
heard she came to India once to do an advanced course in
yoga at some ashram in Poona. She did not bother to get
in touch with me. That was the end of the Betty story.'

'Good story,' says Baig. 'I must tell Sakina Begum when
the servants are not around. She will love it.'

'She must have a very low opinion of me,' says Boota.

'Not at all,' replies Baig, 'she calls you *Rangeela Sardar*—
colourful Sikh.'

∾

In the Orient, footwear is regarded as a symbol of
contempt; it is the lowest thing a person wears and is
often subjected to dust and dirt. One is expected to take
off one's footwear before entering a place of worship, and in
the Indian subcontinent people leave their shoes and
sandals outside the doorstep when they call on friends or
relatives. So it is logical that when men fall out, they
instantly take off their footwear to belabour their
adversary; it is known as *jootey ki pitaaee* (shoe beating). It
is the ultimate form of insult. If the adversary is not
within one's reach or is well guarded, one can achieve the
same result by hurling one's shoe from a distance. This is
what an Iraqi journalist did to President Bush while he
was addressing a press conference in Baghdad. He wanted

to register his protest against Americans invading Iraq on the pretext that it was manufacturing weapons of mass destruction. The American government later admitted that it found no evidence of Iraq being engaged in such nefarious activity.

Hurling shoes to register a protest is expensive. The hurler throws one of his pair of shoes. It is immediately confiscated to become an exhibit at the hurler's trial for assault and battery. He has to buy another pair and keep the lone one as a memento of what he did.

A similar incident took place in Delhi on the 7th of April 2009. At a press conference being addressed by Home Minister P. Chidambaram, a long-bearded young Sikh journalist named Jarnail Singh, working as a reporter for the Hindi newspaper *Dainik Jagran*, hurled one of his shoes at the minister. The fellow was no marksman—he missed his target. He was promptly arrested and fired from his job—as he well deserved. The minister generously forgave him, saying he shared the hurt of the shoe-thrower's community. Jarnail Singh immediately became a hero of the Sikhs. And what is more, though he missed hitting the minister, he hit the bull's eye of the real target he had in mind. He became the chief topic of conversation in the capital and the country. And needless to say, a topic hotly debated by members of the Sunset Club.

April in Delhi is a neither-here-nor-there month. You are not sure if winter and spring are over and summer is there. One day it can be as chilly as in December; the next day it may be like a day in June. Also, one day you may get rain and even a hailstorm, the following week hot desert winds and a dust storm. The weather not only plays games with humans but also with nature. Semuls shed their pods, which burst and cover the ground with blobs of cotton. The palas has its short run of glory and returns to its drab cloak of leaves. Corals follow suit. But jacarandas are out in full bloom, and by the month's end roadsides and roundabouts are ablaze with fiery orange and yellow gulmohars and krishna siris.

The unpredictability of April is beautifully captured by the Sanskrit writer Bhasa in his *Avimaraka, Love's Enchanted World*:

> *How enchanting is the great variety of this world!*
> *Gone is the heat of the day as earth dresses for night;*
> *The evening breeze of this strange world gently the body*
>   *touches*
> *Slowly she removes the sun from her forehead,*
> *Quietly puts around her neck a garland of stars*
> *Scatters the brave throughout the sleeping city*
> *And joins together the bodies of young lovers.*

∾

Baig was looking forward to bringing up the story of the shoe-thrower with his friends. He sensed it would rouse the hackles of both Sharma and Boota as the matter involved conflict between Hindus and Sikhs. And he being Muslim could be a neutral listener. And so it turned out to be.

'Brothers, tell me what provoked the young Sardar journalist to hurl his shoe at the home minister, who had nothing to do with the massacre of Sikhs which took place so many years ago?'

Sharma responds with alacrity: 'Sardars are known to be slow-witted, it takes a long time for them to react to any event. They are also known to be hot-headed: once they lose their cool, they go berserk and hit out at any thing or person within easy reach. I was not a bit surprised when I read about it. I said to myself, all said and done, he is a Sardar.'

Boota feels he must put Sharma in his place. 'Oh Panditji, did it not occur to you that the fellow missed hitting the home minister and yet hit the real target he had in mind? The Congress Party had put up two people who had taken part in the killings of Sikhs as its candidates for parliamentary elections. His act roused the conscience of the people. There were protest meetings all over the country, and the Congress Party has been forced to withdraw the names of both men. Does that sound slow-witted and ill-timed to you?'

There's a lull in the angry exchange between Sharma and Boota, and they begin to cool off. Baig has not had his fill of fun, so he provokes Boota again: 'Bootaji, how long will you harbour this *gussa* against Hindus? Why not forgive and forget?'

'It will be as long as the criminals are not punished!' replies Boota. 'Do you know that of the thousands who went on the rampage against Sikhs, barely twenty have been convicted. We have every right to be angry at the miscarriage of justice. And Hindus go on telling the world that they are a peace-loving people. Give them a chance and see how peaceful they are! You are a Muslim, you should know. How many Muslims have they killed since we gained independence? Tell me.'

'Many thousands,' concedes Baig. 'We have got used to being killed. A few thousands after they pulled down the Babri Masjid; another few thousands after a train compartment caught fire at Godhra railway station. As I said, we have got used to it.'

Sharma feels the two are ganging up against him, so he takes them head-on: 'Bootaji, please tell us how much did you protest when Bhindranwale said every Sikh should kill thirty-four Hindus and his goons went around dragging Hindus from buses and shooting them? Did one Sikh leader say a word against him? No, they were dead scared of him because he thought nothing of having his critics eliminated. And now he is dead, you worship him as a saint and a martyr.' Then he turns to Baig. 'You Muslims wanted Pakistan and got it. And yet more of you are living in India than in Pakistan. If we did what Pakistanis did to Hindus and Sikhs, you would all be driven out of this country. We form over eighty per cent of the population of this country and yet we have a Sikh prime minister, a Sikh head of the Planning Commission, Sikh and Muslim cabinet ministers, chief ministers of states, governors of provinces. And all we get in return is ingratitude. Is this fair, I ask you?'

Sharma knows he has got the better of his friends in the debate. That should have been expected; he is a Brahmin and Brahmins are the brainiest people in the world. As Sharma has often explained in his lectures, India's caste system can be compared to the human body. The head is Brahmin, the arms and torso are Kshatriyas—the fighting types like Rajputs, Marathas, Sikhs. The pelvis and thighs are Vaishyas—the trading castes like Banias and Marwaris who look after the economy of the country. Shudras are the legs and feet on which the body stands. They do menial jobs—they are sweepers, cobblers, removers of carcasses. It is a division based on functions expected to be performed, so the caste system cannot be dismissed as outdated rubbish.

However, having established his mental superiority over his friends, Sharma feels that he must also apply a soothing balm on their hurt feelings, as he cherishes their friendship. 'Chalo ji, let bygones be bygones. They are of no importance to us today. What is important is to speak the truth, no matter what the consequences. Boota, what are those lines about truth that you often quote?'

Quoting other people's words of wisdom is Boota's favourite pastime. He clears his throat and recites:

> *Truth is good*
> *If someone else dies for the truth*
> *It is better*
> *You are no martyr who should*
> *On the gallows be hung*
> *Hold your tongue.*

5

MAY OF THE
LABURNUMS

In Delhi, May can be scorchingly hot. Those who can
afford fans, air coolers and air conditioners stay indoors;
those who can't, seek trees which have cool shade. Some
die of sun or heat stroke. Some get prickly heat round
their necks and just learn to suffer it.

Though heat and dust make life out of doors hell, there
are spells of respite. Out of the blue, grey clouds arrive
and it begins to drizzle. This year, there were two
drizzles—one on the 2nd of May, and a few days later, the
second one. On the 10th of May there was a dust storm
which swept across the city with gale force, knocking

down banyan, neem and jamun trees. Then came rain. Stormy winds sent raindrops skywards several times, till the drops turned into hailstones. They came down like pebbles hurled by Indra, lord of the skies, on cars parked in the open, on tarmac roads and lawns. For a few moments it looked as if the city had had a snowfall. The temperature came down and people rejoiced on the streets. The next day it became a distant memory as the blazing sun reasserted its right to scorch the earth. But hope of relief came with the thought that the south-west monsoons had reached the Andamans. A week later the monsoon reached Kerala. On the last day of the month, Delhi got its first pre-monsoon shower.

The one thing that makes May in Delhi memorable is the flowering of laburnums. There are lots of them along the city roads. People don't notice them because most of the year they are nondescript middle-sized trees with long black seed pods hanging down from the branches. Then suddenly flowers appear: a mass of canary gold dripping down like bunches of Kandahar grapes. You gape open-mouthed at this miracle of beauty. No fragrance, only gaudy showers of gold. Their glory lasts barely a week or ten days. Then they return to their drab existence. They make a second attempt to flower at the onset of the monsoon but it is not the same thing.

࿇

Boota is looking out of his window to see if there are any girls, boys or their pet dogs playing on the lawn facing his window. It is too early, the sun is still too hot for them to step out. He catches sight of the laburnum in full bloom. How is it that he had not noticed it last year? He steps out of his flat to take a better look. In all its golden splendour, it proclaims the glory of God. He must tell his friends about it. Unfortunately few of his countrymen show much interest in trees, birds or animals—they are far more interested in politics, money, scandals or religion. And so it turned out to be that evening, when the Sunset Club met.

'Have you seen the laburnums in bloom?' Boota asks as soon as they are seated on the Boorha Binch.

'Laburnums? What are they?' asks Sharma.

'Yellow flowers now in bloom along the roads.'

'You mean amaltas? Yes I noticed some.'

Baig is equally indifferent: 'I see them on my way here. But they have no fragrance. What is a flower without fragrance? It is like a good-looking woman without character. We have motia—jasmine. My Begum picks them every morning and puts them in a silver bowl full of water. The whole room is filled with the scent of jasmine. I suspect there's a hidden reason for your love for amaltas—it's because it is a powerful laxative. And you need a stomach cleanser every day.'

Sharma adds: 'You two come into the park from the wrong entrance. Come over the old stone bridge and breathe in the fragrance of maulsari, though you can hardly see the tiny flower. Right now they are at their best.'

After a few minutes' pause, Boota turns to Baig and asks: 'When did you last see the moon?'

'Strange question. Why do you ask?'

'Because I have not seen it or the stars for many years. There was a time we used to sleep on our rooftops or on lawns with mosquito nets, revolving fans, earthenware surahis with steel tumblers over their mouth. We saw the moon in all its phases, from a crescent to *Pooran Masi*, full moon, and then to moonless *Amavasya*. We saw Venus and the Pole Star and the Sapt Rishi—the Plough. And could tell the time without looking at our watches. Now, all that is in the past.'

'You are right, Bootaji,' says Baig. 'If you are missing the moon and the stars so much, all you have to do is to spend a night in a village half an hour's drive from Delhi.'

Sharma cuts in impatiently, 'You are obsessed with flowering trees and moonlit nights when the country is beset with the prospect of another Kurukshetra. No one talks of anything besides the general elections which will decide the future of the country for decades to come. You should take life more seriously.'

Boota does not like to be scolded. 'Okay, Panditji, tell us about Kurukshetra. Who are the Pandavas and the

Kauravas in the electoral battle? On whose side is Shri Krishna this time?'

Baig interrupts: 'Please explain what are Pandavas and Kauravas to me. All I know is Kurukshetra is a town in Haryana regarded as sacred by the Hindus.'

Sharma explains: 'It is sacred because it is here that the battle between the cousins was fought. And it was here that Shri Krishna propounded the Bhagavad Gita, which is to Hindus like the holy Koran is to Muslims and the Bible to Christians. He tells us what is right and what is wrong; how one should do one's duty regardless of its consequences, and of the odds against one. It is one of the world's greatest books. I read a passage or two from it every day.'

'It also supports the caste system,' says Boota in a sarcastic tone.

'It does not,' says Sharma in a tone of authority.

'Yes, it does,' persists Boota. 'It says when castes intermingle, there is chaos.'

'You've got it all wrong,' says Sharma angrily. 'In the Gita castes mean qualities not accident of birth. Read it more carefully—and without bias.'

Baig acts the peacemaker. 'Let's forget what the Gita says about castes. Let us decide which side in the battle to come is in the right and should win; and which will harm the country and should be defeated.'

'The most wonderful thing about the election is that it has been left to the people to decide which side are the Pandavas and which the Kauravas, and which has Shri Krishna's blessings,' says Sharma.

'Don't make it sound like a holy war,' cuts in Boota. 'The main issue is simple—one side is for Hindutva, to make India a Hindu Rashtra. The other wants it to remain secular and above religious differences. I see it as a fight between Hindu fundoos and Gandhi's followers. Hindu supporters are the RSS, Hindu Mahasabha, Shiv Sena, Bajrang Dal, led by the BJP nominee for prime minister, L.K. Advani. The Gandhiites are led by Sonia Gandhi, her son Rahul and their nominee, Prime Minister Manmohan Singh. Perhaps I am oversimplifying the issue but I think that is how the *aam aadmi*, the common man, sees it.'

'You confuse me even more than before,' says Baig. 'I will ask my Begum. She takes more interest in *siyasat*— politics—than I do.'

'Yes, please do. And tell us tomorrow what she says.' Sharma stands up to leave. The other two also get up and bid each other goodnight.

'So, what did your Begum Sahiba have to say about our prime minister?' asks Sharma as soon as they are on the Boorha Binch the following evening.

'Many things,' replies Baig. 'She says Manmohan Singh is able and honest, he has never made money dishonestly nor done favours to members of his family or friends. He never praises himself or runs down his detractors. He does not talk too much—not like other politicians who talk *bakwaas* all the time.' After a pause Baig adds: 'What seems to have made my wife more enamoured of Manmohan Singh is she heard him reading out a speech on TV. His head moved from right to left and she shouted, "He is reading Urdu."'

All the three have a hearty laugh.

Baig continues: 'She said Manmohan made the ideal leader of a *kaarwaan* and quoted a couplet from Iqbal about the qualities of a *mir-e-kaarwaan*—leader of a caravan:

Nigaah buland, sukhan dil nawaaz, jaan pur soz
Yehi hai rakht-e-safar mir-e-kaarwaan ke liye.

'She translated it as: "Lofty vision, heart-warming speech, love that conquers all hearts." That is what the aam aadmi thinks of Manmohan Singh.'

Sharma bides his patience for a while before he puts his next question: 'That is all very well; he made a good professor of economics. But is that good enough to be made prime minister of the world's largest democracy? A prime minister has to be elected to the Lok Sabha. As I've pointed out to you before, he fought one Lok Sabha election and lost. They had to get him a flat in Gauhati and Assamese MPs to elect him to the Rajya Sabha. A puppet is not acceptable to our people as prime minister. That is what L.K. Advani says. I think he has a point. He is the nominee of Sonia Gandhi and her son, Rahul. Sonia knows that people won't accept a foreign-born PM. And Rahul is doing the most important job of keeping the Congress alive. The mother and son duo have found an unambitious, good man to hold the fort for them.'

'The aam aadmi is aware of all that,' adds Boota. 'Did the Begum Sahiba say anything about Advani who is proclaiming himself as the prime minister-in-waiting?'

Baig pauses before answering, 'She is against him. She says he demolished the Babri Masjid. Who will forgive him for this sin? She says they should rename the BJP as the MTP—the Masjid Torh Party!'

'That is also the opinion of the aam aadmi,' says Boota. 'The Hindus have never forgiven Muslims for the many temples they demolished centuries ago. How can Muslims and fair-minded Hindus forgive Advani and company for a crime he committed only seventeen years ago? Baig Sahib, that makes this electoral conflict a Kurukshetra of our times.'

∾

Saturday, the 16th of May 2009 is like other 16th of Mays of years past: the sun comes up at 5.43 a.m., determined to make it as hot a day as any in the month. Being the weekend, fewer people than usual go to work. In any event, they have more important things to think of. The nation's future is to be announced that day. Of course, their future had already been sealed in ballot boxes across the country; what is to be revealed on the 16th is the will of the people sealed within the ballot boxes. So every household that has a radio or TV set sits glued to it to know what is in store for them. So it is in the homes of Sharma, Boota and Baig. Television sets are switched on early in the morning, with members of their family, and the servants and their families clustered around them. Sharma, typically, takes a dispassionate view of the results. His sister, who took her servants with her to the polling booth and made sure they voted for the Hindu party, is deeply involved. As results start coming in, she becomes distraught. 'What is going on?' she asks her brother.

'Nothing, just the results,' he answers.

'Are we handing over our country to the Sikhs? Can't we Hindus run our own country?'

Sharma replies in a grim tone, 'No need to get worked up. Sikhs are Hindus with long hair and beards. Nothing different.'

'You tell a Sikh he is Hindu and hear what he says,' says his sister. 'He goes off his head *jab uskey baara bajtey hain.*'

Sharma protests mildly, 'Don't use such language, just watch the results.'

Boota is armed with paper and pen to note down the results as they are announced. Baig, who is looking through his account books, prefers to get the results second-hand.

By noon it becomes clear that the Congress Party led by Sonia Gandhi, her son Rahul and Prime Minister Manmohan Singh is heading towards a decisive victory, and the saffron Hindu parties led by Advani, the BJP candidate for prime ministership, are in for a drubbing. By the evening Advani concedes he has lost and is going to step down from the leadership of the BJP.

The news is received in the homes of members of the Sunset Club in different ways. Sharma is upset that the Hindu parties have fared so poorly and that there will not be a viable Opposition in Parliament. He ponders over the future of Indian democracy. Boota has no such misgivings: he treats the results as a personal victory and rewards himself with three large helpings of his favourite single malt Scotch. At Baig's residence the Begum Sahiba is overjoyed. 'Shabash,' she exclaims, and scoffs at Advani: '*Mazaa chakhaa diya*—serves you right. *Aur torh masjidein, nikamma kahin ka*—go break some more mosques, you useless, good-for-nothing man! And you dare call our Manmohan *nikamma*!'

The next morning Sharma is calm, as is expected of him as a philosopher-civil servant. Boota is in poor shape. He has a terrible hangover and he is more constipated than usual. He makes many attempts to relieve himself but to no avail. In the afternoon he looks for his glycerine suppositories in the fridge where he usually keeps them. He can't find them. In desperation, he uses his index finger and inserts it in his rectum to open a passage for the accumulated shit. It has become hard as cement and all he gets is a soiled finger. He tries it three times with no success. He gives up and sits back in his armchair, not knowing what to do. Then suddenly pressure builds up in his belly. He is back on the commode. This time his bowels open up with a loud explosion, like a cork popping out of a bottle of champagne. The turd comes out like balls from an elephant's bottom. He gets up and examines the full toilet bowl with satisfaction. His head stops throbbing and he dozes off for almost an hour, waking just in time to catch up with his friends in Lodhi Gardens.

Baig notices his sallow complexion and slower pace. 'Bootaji, you look as if you have been celebrating the election results all night!'

'I have,' replies Boota, 'and paying the price. I have been sick all day.'

'Learn moderation,' advises Sharma. 'Elections come and go. One party of corrupt politicians loses, another party of corrupt politicians wins. Nothing really changes.'

'You are hundred per cent correct,' says Baig. 'For the last many months I have heard nothing besides elections,

elections, elections, as if there was nothing else left in the world to talk about. Let us agree that from this evening we will not talk about elections any more. Give me your hands.'

Sharma and Boota put out their palms to be slapped by Baig and reply, 'Agreed. No more elections.'

6

MONTH OF THE SCORCHER

It is said hell is a very hot place. If you want a foretaste of what may be your fate, you should spend the month of June in Delhi. The night before the month began there was rain. Dilliwalas awoke to a gentle, cool breeze laden with the fragrance of the first raindrops on parched earth. 'This can't be the monsoon,' they say, 'but it is on its way to Delhi. If it is pouring in Kerala, it will not be too long before it reaches us.' It was an illusion. June 2009 was as long and tedious as any in years past. Temperatures hovered between 40 and 43 degrees—day after day, including on the longest day of the year, the summer solstice of the 21st of June. Guru Nanak summed up the agony of June in his *Baramasi*:

In Ashadh the sun scorches
Skies are hot
The earth burns like an oven
Waters give up their vapours
But it burns and scorches relentlessly
Thus the land fails not
To fulfil its destiny

The scene is not as bleak as it appears at first sight. June may be hot as hell but it also ushers in the season of mangoes, the very best in the world. Indians are passionately fond of mangoes. It is said that the greatest Urdu poet and the pride of Delhi, Mirza Asadullah Khan Ghalib, ate a dozen every day. One day a friend who was not particularly enamoured of the fruit was sitting with him when a donkey happened to pass by. It sniffed the leftovers of a heap of discarded mango skins and seed stones and walked away. The friend remarked: 'See Mirza, even a donkey does not care for mangoes.' Ghalib, who was known for his ready wit, replied, 'Yes, it is only donkeys who don't like mangoes.'

There are nearly two thousand varieties of mangoes, ranging from the humble pea-sized to the melon-sized, each with a distinct flavour. The most pricey are Alphonsos from Konkan, and they are the only ones which are exported. However, Dilliwalas prefer those grown in western Uttar Pradesh—Dussehris, Langdas, Chausas and Ratauls. Baig, besides owning a lot of real estate in Delhi, also has a large mango orchard near Lucknow. He does not bother to market his fruit. Instead, he sends basketfuls to his friends, and has plenty left for his family and staff. Among the recipients of his bounty are Pandit Sharma and Sardar Boota Singh.

Sharma loves mangoes but his sister, who does all the buying of fruit and vegetables for the house, thinks they cost too much; she only buys bananas. Baig's mangoes are the only ones they get to savour through the summer. Boota also relishes mangoes. Some of his rich Bombay friends send him Alphonsos. By the time he is finished with one large basketful, another arrives. He never has to buy any. But he has to guard against eating too many, and rations himself to one in the afternoon. They are said to be laxative and he can do with mild laxatives because of his chronic constipation. But he also has problems with blood sugar and incipient diabetes. So his motto is a mango a day keeps the doctor away.

Baig has no problems enjoying the produce of his orchard. Nor does anyone else in his household. So every afternoon buckets full of mangoes cooled in water are brought into the large reception room and everyone takes his fill. No plates, knives or spoons, mangoes are best eaten with one's hands—tear the skin off by biting into it, take the rest in your fingers and savour the sweet, succulent flesh, then suck the large seed, the *guthlee*, to the bone. A large empty basket is beside them. They toss mango skins and guthlees in it. The last act of the mango feast is the washing of hands and rinsing of mouth.

The mango is a messy fruit to eat. That is one reason citizens of the Indian subcontinent are about the only people who relish it and call it the king of fruits.

The month drags on and on with the scorching sun and unbearable heat. Our three characters spend their days in air-cooled rooms and only venture out to Lodhi Gardens late in the evenings for some fresh, warm air and chit-chat. On the 30th of June there is a welcome shower in the morning and the dry hot air turns into humid hot air. Boota and Baig arrive at the same time. After waiting for Sharma and wondering 'What happened to Panditji?', they relax. He is censorious and they don't come out with stories of the exploits of their younger days before him. When they feel Sharma is not likely to come Baig asks Boota, 'Tell me of the most unusual encounter you had with a woman, chondee-chondee—dripping with sex.'

Boota has often thought about it and still cannot believe it really happened. He recounts: 'I haven't told you that at one time, besides working for newspapers, I occasionally conducted parties of foreign tourists to Agra to see the Taj Mahal. Since I had written a booklet on the historical monuments of Agra and could speak English, the Government of India's tourist department occasionally asked me to conduct VIPs to Agra. It paid well—a thousand rupees and all hotel expenses. That was a lot of money in those days. This must have been many years ago, when I was still in my forties. General Eisenhower, the president of the United States, came on an official visit to India. There was a large party of journalists with him. Our tourism minister offered them a free visit to the Taj and asked me to escort them. A plane was chartered to fly them there and back. I did my best to tell them about Agra, Shahjahan and the Taj Mahal but the buggers were not in the least interested. When we got to the Taj all they could say was, "Jeez! That's something! How much did it cost?" I tried to convert rupees into dollars. They were not impressed. "How long did it take the king, the guy who built it?" I was disgusted. And we flew back to Delhi in the afternoon in time for a press conference on Indo-American relations.'

'Nothing chondee-chondee about that,' says Baig. 'You didn't make up to a woman journalist?'

'Arrey bhai, wait, I am coming to the sequel. The next afternoon I went to the tourism office to collect my fees. There was an Indian woman there; fiftyish, plump, wearing thick glasses. She spoke English like a memsahib. I noticed she had a steel bangle on her right wrist, and a small kirpan dangling by the side. I presumed she was a Sikh living in England. As I collected my fees, she asked me, "Are you a tourist guide?" I replied, "Yes madam, when I have free time I show foreign visitors round Agra."

'"What do you charge?" she asked me.

'"Rs 1,000 and all hotel expenses."

'"Are you free tomorrow to show me the Taj?"

'I paused—she was not appetizing and I did not like her bossiness. For some reason I said, "We will have to stay overnight in Agra. There is a lot more to see in the city."

'"That's all right with me. We can stay the night but all I want is to see the Taj. I am not interested in other monuments. You want to be paid in advance?" she asked.

'"No madam. After the visit will be okay."

'"I am staying at the Ashoka Hotel. Please get there by 8 a.m. I have hired an AC taxi for the duration of the visit. I'd like to leave early as I don't like fast driving and I can see the countryside. Is that all right?"

'"Yes madam," I replied.

'Baig, I really wanted to call off the deal but that snobbish Sikhni intrigued me. So next morning I dutifully reported at the Ashoka on the dot of 8 a.m. She was waiting on the steps of the main entrance, with a Mercedes-Benz taxi and liveried chauffeur. I greeted her with *"Sat Sri Akal"* to convey to her that I knew she was Sikh like me. She simply nodded her head. I took the front seat beside the chauffeur while she occupied the rear seat. And we set off—out of Delhi, past Faridabad. When I turned back to tell her about the places we were driving through, she was reading from a pocket *gutka*—prayer book. Even when we came to Sikandra and I asked her if she would like to see Akbar's tomb, she shook her head and replied, "No, I just want to see the Taj."

'So we got to Agra, and to a five-star hotel near the Taj. She booked two rooms next to each other. It was lunchtime. She ordered her meal to be served in her room, and ordered me, "3.30 for the Taj."

'The hotel people knew me and did not charge me for my food or drinks as I often brought foreign tourists to them. So I had my beer and lunch in the restaurant, rested for a while in my room and at exactly 3.30, I was waiting for her, chatting with the chauffeur. "Chalo," she said, speaking Hindustani for the first time. I opened the rear door for her and took my seat next to the driver. A couple of minutes later we arrived at the Taj. In those days there were no entrance charges so we just went through the gate. She stopped to gaze at the snow-white marble mausoleum. "Beautiful!" she said. "Now I can tell everyone in England I've seen the Taj."

'We walked up to the main building. The steps were too high for her so she asked me to lend her a hand. I took her hand, warm and clammy, and helped her up the stairs. I took her inside and showed her the two tombs and around the building. "I am tired," she said. "Anywhere we can sit down for a while?" I took her to the rear where there was a stone bench and you got a view of the Yamuna and the countryside across the river.

'"You speak English very well," she said. "Where did you pick it up?"

'"In England," I replied.

'"What were you doing in England?" she asked.

'"I was in college," I replied.

'I can't tell you how suddenly the woman's attitude changed. "I am sorry I did not realize this," she said. "I thought you were just a government tourist guide. Why do you do this?"

'"It's fun once in a while. Get to meet interesting people. Lots of middle-aged women. Very friendly."

'"You have fun with them?"

'"Some; they ask for it."

'"Do you charge them extra for it?"

'"Madam, I am not a gigolo. But they leave me presents. Mainly ballpoint pens. I have quite a collection of Parkers, Mont Blancs and Cross pens."

'She seemed disgusted. But she had to take my hand again going down the steps. She also asked me to sit beside her on the rear seat. By the time we got back to the hotel, it was dark. She ordered dinner to be served in her room an hour later, after she had said her evening prayers. I went to the bar and ordered a large single malt and soda. Then a second one. Had a hefty meal—beef steak and French wine followed by a cognac. All on the house. I was quite tipsy by the time I went to the reception desk and asked for my room key. The fellow looked up at the board with room keys and said, "Sir, it seems the madam you are escorting has taken the keys of both rooms."

'To say the least I was foxed. Why on earth had she taken my key? Had I to go and beg her to get into my own bedroom? Anyhow, when I got to her room I found the door ajar. I pushed it open. She was lying in bed, with the table lamp on. Without her glasses, she looked less forbidding. She spread out her bare arms and said, "Come! Shut the door behind you." I did as ordered and went to her bedside. "Lie with me for a while," she ordered. Those days I could get an erection without bothering about what the woman looked like. I pulled down my trousers and lay beside her. She was stark naked. "Not even your kachha?" I asked. "No, not even my kachha or kirpan. Smear some cream on your thing, I am dry." I smeared the cream lying beside her table lamp on my

laura. I entered her. She intoned, "*Wahguru*," and shut her
eyes. You know, when you are not emotionally involved
with a woman you can hold out much longer than with
one you love. Longer if you are drunk.

'So it seemed to go on for an eternity. After what
seemed an hour, I felt her shudder beneath me, and
scream, "*Hai mar gayee!* Wahguru! Wahguru!" I pumped
my seed into her hairy cunt. She was flattened out and
murmured, "That was nice, now you can go to sleep."

'My room key was on the table by the bedside lamp. I
put on my trousers and staggered to my room. I was too
tired to wash and change into my night pajamas. No
sooner had I put my head on the pillow, I was lost to the
world. Baig, you will find it hard to believe, I did not even
know her full name—just Miss Singh. Neither did she
bother to ask me my name. I was just Mr Singh, the
tourist guide.

'The next morning we drove back to Delhi. Though we
sat next to each other on the rear seat, she was busy
reading her gutka. She dropped me at Connaught Place and
said, "It was nice knowing you." She gave me a sealed
envelope bearing the name of the Agra hotel and said,
"Your fee, and thanks again." She got back to her hotel
and took the night flight back to London. It was only back
in my flat that I tore open the envelope. It had two
thousand rupees—one thousand for my fee as a guide,

and one thousand for my services. I never heard from her again—I have no idea whether she is alive or dead.'

'So she did treat you like a gigolo,' remarks Baig.

'Not a bad profession,' replies Boota, 'provided the gigolo can choose his woman, and not the other way round!'

ᘯ

It is the end of June and so far it has rained only three days in the month. 'What has happened to the *kambakht* monsoon?' asks Baig.

'Vagaries of nature,' replies Pandit Sharma gravely. 'Some years it rains too much and we have floods and villages are washed away. Some years there is very little rain and we have drought. But people don't die of hunger in India these days. We have canals and tube wells to irrigate our fields. We have huge reserves of wheat and rice which are put in the market or given away at throw-away prices.'

Baig is not convinced. 'Take it from me, if it does not rain soon there will be *kahat*—famine. My Begum says so. She is stocking up grain and rice and pickles against the eventuality.'

They fall silent for some time.

A flock of black and white birds flies overhead and perches on the top of trees, calling to each other. 'You know these birds?' asks Boota. 'They come all the way from Africa, taking advantage of monsoon winds, and usually arrive at our western shores by early June. It is known as the monsoon bird; it is the *megha papeeha*, harbinger of the monsoon. So don't lose hope.'

7

CRY OF THE PEACOCK

In July, monsoon clouds cover Delhi's skies. Stormy moisture-laden winds shake trees and send their branches swirling like dancing dervishes. There is lightning, thunder and rain. People run out into the streets to get drenched and dance in the rain. In parks and gardens, peacocks fan out their tails, their wings palpitate with lust, they strut around their chosen peahens, raise their heads to the sky and scream *paon, paon*.

July 2009 begins with grey clouds spread over the city. People look up longingly and pray for rain. Not a drop falls. However, all the three members of the Sunset Club decide not to take any chances against a heavy downpour and give their evening tryst in Lodhi Gardens a miss.

ॐ

On the 2nd of July, the Delhi High Court pronounces a verdict that hereafter sodomy by mutual consent will no longer be a punishable crime. It is nothing new for the Western world where even gay marriages have been legalized, but it remains unacceptable in the Orient, particularly in Islamic countries. It is also not acceptable to most religious-minded people, be they Hindu, Muslim, Christian or Sikh; nor even to the common man in the street, though he himself may have indulged in *laundebaazi*—making love to boys. Any adult who has access to women and yet continues to engage in sex with his own gender is known as *gandoo*—bugger.

On the 3rd of July, the Delhi High Court judgment makes headline news in all the national dailies, and is the top item on all TV channels. They carry interviews with celebrities, soliciting their opinions. It is the topic of debate at the Sunset Club meeting that evening.

'What do you make of the high court judgment permitting homosexuality?' asks Baig, as the three are seated.

'I think it is a mistake, a big mistake,' says Sharma. 'It is against the order of nature, all religions forbid it as sinful. We simply follow the West, so as to be counted amongst advanced nations. No doubt Boota will disagree with me.'

'I do,' says Boota. 'Homosexuality is not against the order of nature, as you say. Making it into a crime by man-made laws is against the law of nature. When sexual urges manifest themselves they find whatever outlet they can. All of us go through a phase of homosexuality. Most get over it when they get access to women. However, a minority remain homosexual and call themselves Gay. If you look carefully, it exists among animals as well. I have noticed it among young dogs and monkeys. Sharmaji, your Dabboos must have tried to hump your legs. Am I wrong?'

Baig ponders over the matter and says, 'I agree with Boota that all of us pass through a phase of homosexuality. Maybe that is the order of nature. But why then do all religions condemn it? Remember, the Bible has the story of Sodom and Gomorrah. The Koran also condemns it. I don't know about what Hinduism or Sikhism have to say on the subject. Sharmaji, you must know.'

Before Sharma can respond, Boota says, 'The answer is simple. At the time these religions were founded, all countries were sparsely populated, and people were exhorted to multiply. Now many countries, especially ours, are grossly overpopulated; we can't afford to multiply any more. Legalizing homosexuality will make a marginal difference.'

'By this logic, the state should also provide brothels in all mohallas. Men can have all the sex they want and satisfy their lust without adding to the population,' says Baig.

'I am for legalizing prostitution,' says Boota. 'All brothels should have condom-vending machines, provide weekly medical check-ups for prostitutes and a reasonable pension for them from fifty onwards. No pimps, no fleecing by the police.' He has a look of triumph on his face. 'Baig, what do you have to say?'

'I am confused,' admits Baig. 'In my boyhood I fooled around with boys, later some whores as well. But now I am a happily married man and think both buggery and whoring are bad. So I keep my mouth shut.'

It is getting late. Their servants come and plead with them to get home. '*Sahib, bahut machhar hai*—mosquitoes are biting us.' It is true, the servants are not as well clad as their masters. They all get up. Sharma is worried about what he will tell his sister when she asks what they talked about. He will not be able to tell her what Boota said. It is the same with Baig. He cannot repeat Boota's opinions favouring buggery and prostitution. His Begum would explode and ask, 'Have you nothing better to talk about than dirty things?' Both Baig and Sharma have to make up something to keep the women calm. Only Boota is pleased with himself. He must polish up his ideas and put them across in his columns. He loves to provoke his readers and make them react by writing letters to editors—double publicity.

❧

We are ten days into July and there is no sign of the monsoon. Perhaps it will arrive on the first of *Sawan* which falls on the 16th. We believe the Vikrami calendar to be closer to the seasons than the Roman. Sawan arrives but lets us down. However, five days later there is a shower. Our hopes revive. Girls make swings under trees, sing songs about meetings of lovers. Boys fly kites from rooftops.

Indian poets have written more on the season of rains than on any other topic. Here are a couple of examples. Amaru (ninth century AD) writes of the prelude:

The summer sun, who robbed the pleasant nights,
And plundered all the water of the rivers,
And burned the earth, and scorched the forest-trees
Is now in hiding; and the black clouds,
Spread thick across the sky to track him down,
Hunt for the criminal with lightning flashes.

Yogeshvara (first century AD) has this beautiful description of peacocks dancing:

With tail-fans spread, and undulating wings
With whose vibrating pulse the air now sings,
Their voices lifted and their beaks stretched wide,
Treading the rhythmic dance from side to side,
Eyeing the rain cloud's dark, majestic hue,

Richer in colour than their own throats' blue
With necks upraised, to which their tails advance,
Now in the rains the screaming peacocks dance.

∾

On the last day of the month, Sharma fails to turn up. Baig asks Boota, 'What happened to Panditji? I hope he is well.'

'Nothing wrong with him,' Boota replies. 'He rang me up this morning. He likes to go to shraadhs, havans and condolence meetings. He does not tell me about them lest I think he is superstitious. I suppose he has gone to attend some such function.'

Sharma's absence gives Boota the opportunity to know more about Baig's past. 'Baig, you made me tell you about the most bizarre sexual encounters I had and I told you all I remembered in great detail. Now it is your turn to tell me of another one of yours—the most bizarre one. It is only fair.'

Baig ponders over the request. 'It would be better if you did not ask me. I have done something which I am too ashamed to admit. If anyone got to know about it, my face would be blackened forever. I am sure if my Begum got to know she would never talk to me again, perhaps ask for talaq.'

Boota's curiosity increases. 'It's not about some murder you committed that I want to know—only about your sexual encounter. I promise to keep it to myself,' he assures Baig.

'You swear by God? Put your hand on your heart and say my tongue be clipped if I tell anyone about it.'

Boota puts his right hand on his chest and says, 'May my tongue be clipped if I reveal Baig Sahib's secret to anyone.'

Baig puts his head back and shuts his eyes. 'Well, it is like this. My father has a cousin a few years younger than him. He owns hundreds of acres of land not far from Bareilly. He is married to my mother's cousin who is a lot younger than him and my mother. They had no children and treated me as if I was their adopted son. His only interest in life was shikar. During the winter season he was out from the early hours of the morning, shooting duck in *jheels*. When the sun came up, he shot partridges, quails, doves and starlings. After the midday meal he went after deer. He returned home late in the evening, his jeep stacked with what he had shot. I used to spend my winter days with him and often accompanied him on shikars. I enjoyed myself in their home and thought of it as my own. Every night my aunt—mausi, as I called her—brought me a glass of milk laced with almonds and saffron. Delicious! What was more delicious is that before leaving she would kiss my forehead, and while doing so, her breasts would brush my nose. Some nights she kissed me twice or thrice and my nose felt the soft touch of her bosom. That gave me bad thoughts about her. I got erections. I did my best to put bad thoughts about her out of my mind. After all, she was my mausi and called me beta—son.

'Fate conspired against me. On one of my visits, my uncle had left for shikar, for a distant jungle in the foothills. This time, he did not take me along. On the very first night, when my aunt brought me my glass of milk she bolted the door from inside. After kissing my forehead, she kissed me on the lips. I was wild with frenzy. I pulled her into my bed. I was barely fourteen and had never slept with a woman. She directed my member inside her. I went for her like a maniac and pumped gallons of my seed into her. She stayed on. A few minutes later I was at it again. I must have done it to her at least six times—each time longer than the last. We finished just before dawn. I got up at mid-morning, had a hot bath and some breakfast. Then I went to the garden to bask in the sun. She asked me if I had slept well. "Like a log," I replied in English. "Take some more rest after lunch," she advised. "You will need it." I guessed what was on her mind. She spent the next two nights doing the same thing without giving a thought to what the consequences could be.

'I stayed on in Bareilly a week after my uncle returned from shikar. He was very pleased with his success, having shot deer and wild boar and dozens of partridges. He talked about it all the time. I got back to Delhi and rejoined school. It must have been a couple of months later that my Bareilly uncle wrote to my father giving him the good news that after eight years of marriage his wife was expecting a child. My parents were very pleased at the news. There was a lot of property involved and it was good to have an heir to inherit it. Seven months later, my Bareilly mausi came to Delhi to stay with her parents for the delivery. It was a son. There was a lot of rejoicing in our extended family. Now Boota Singhji, if you repeat a word of my story to anyone, I swear by the name of Allah I will kill you.'

'Baig Sahib, don't worry. I will not break my word. But all said and done, lots of men begin their sex lives bedding their aunts, cousins or maidservants. Nothing unusual about it. But tell me, what do you call the *haramzada*, bastard—*Chhota Bhai*, little cousin, or *Beta*, son?'

So July drew to a close with just a couple of short showers and people talked of severe drought and famine. To confirm their fears that worse was to follow, there was a solar eclipse on the 22nd of July. It was the longest in duration that many people had seen, and in some parts of the country, like a total blackout. In a country where ninety-nine per cent of the populace, including its lady president, most ministers of the government and chief ministers of states, believe in astrology, this was enough to cast gloom from the Himalayas down to Kanyakumari.

Baig enjoys Sharma and Boota going for each other on issues on which they are at variance. He is sure the solar eclipse is going to be one of them as they get together on the 22nd evening. Baig casually brings it up and asks Sharmaji, 'You must know a lot about astrology; you think a total solar eclipse forebodes evil?'

Sharma pronounces, 'Astronomy is a science first studied in ancient India. They knew all about the movement of the sun, moon, stars and about lunar and solar eclipses. Astrology as a science was developed by them later.'

As expected, Boota blows his fuse. 'Astronomy is a science but astrology is not a science. It is simple hocus-pocus. Only chootias believe in it. Unfortunately there is no shortage of chootias in our country. Most Hindus have horoscopes cast at birth; they call it *janampatri*. They preserve them and occasionally have them interpreted by pandits. All very vague generalities, many of them meaningless and wrong. Then we have a Bhrigu Samhita which is said to have everyone's life recorded in it. And *bhavishya vanis*—future forecasts—periodically fabricated to suit one's own purpose. And much else. Fortune tellers, palmists flourish in the country. Papers carry columns on what the stars foretell: Aries, Virgo, Leo, Scorpio, etc., etc. There is absolutely nothing to it. Baig Sahib, if I had my way I'd put all the astrologers, palmists, *vaastu* experts, tarot card readers and others behind bars.'

'Calm down, Boota Singh,' says Sharma. 'And do not pronounce judgement on issues about which you know nothing. What do you know about astrology?'

'Nothing, because there is nothing to know,' retorts Boota. 'But you are a sabjantawala. You recall the *Ashta Graha* in 1963 when eight planets were in conjunction? All the astrologers predicted the end of the world. Hundreds of crores went up in smoke as the superstitious organized havans and fed the fires with pure ghee. Trains went empty, planes flew empty, babus did not go to their offices. Life came to a standstill. What happened? Nothing. Absolutely nothing. Only, the rest of the world laughed at us. Sharmaji, tell me if what I am saying is wrong?'

'I don't remember the details,' replies Sharma. 'I certainly did not abstain from work. The attendance in offices was poor but some of us did our duty.'

Boota resumes his diatribe. 'What do you make of auspicious time and *Rahu Kalam*—inauspicious hours— when Saturn is up to some mischief? Chief ministers don't come to office till Rahu Kalam is over. Jayalalitha, who is riddled with superstition, adds another "a" to her name to become Jayalalithaa. To what effect? And the writer Shobha Dé, now married a third time, preaches the virtues of monogamy and adds an "a" to her name to become Shobhaa. Baig, does any of this make sense to you?'

Baig turns peacemaker. 'Bhai Boota, all of us have a few superstitions. Don't single out Hindus. I am sure you must be having your own. We Muslims don't go in for horoscopes but we too have astrologers, *najoomi*s. Some believe in them, others do not.'

The debate on the occult remains inconclusive.

8

NOTHING TO CELEBRATE IN AUGUST

August is one of the four months known as *Chaturmasa,* beginning with the full moon of July called *Gurupurva,* and ending with the full moon night following Diwali. During these three months Lord Vishnu, Preserver of Life, descends to the bottom of the ocean and goes into deep slumber. This period is called *Pralaya*—chaos. It is wise not to celebrate during this time. No Hindu marriage takes place during Chaturmasa.

The rainy season is at its height in August. The skies are overcast and there is a shower or two every other day. At times it rains continuously for three or four days. This is when frogs, who live in muddy ponds and stagnant pools in our parks, really find their voice. Of all animal and bird noises, that of frogs is the most difficult to reproduce in words. The Greek poet Aristophanes got close to it in his play *The Frogs*, where the noise is described as *brek-ek-ek, koax, koax, brek-ek-ek koax!* The simple Americanism— *Newark! Newark!*—could do for the song of the single croaking frog.

August 2009 was different. In the first week there was not a drop of rain, and no chorus of croaking frogs. Clouds came and went, the air was damp, the atmosphere unwholesome. Mosquitoes, flies, cockroaches multiplied, to add to human misery. Delhi's lifeline, the river Yamuna, usually bursts its banks in August and on days looks like a sea. It assumes its earlier incarnation of Triyama, sister of Yama, Lord of Death, and sweeps away villages along its banks, drowning humans and cattle. This year, its waters began to rise in the first week of August, flushing away the excreta and filth that Dilliwalas dump into it. If you don't believe me, take a trip to Okhla where a barrage accumulates its water, to pour some into the Yamuna Canal which takes off from there. It used to be a favourite picnic spot. Now the fetid smell of human shit is all-pervasive.

After a couple of showers, Delhi's woes multiply. Ants and snakes are flushed out of their holes. Some people get bitten to death. Rats and mice invade homes as they have nowhere else to go. Incidence of malaria and dengue fever increases. The change of atmosphere also afflicts some people, among them Boota Singh. Every change of season brings on sneezing, sore throat, running nose, cough and phlegm. No matter that he takes pills of Vitamin C, doses of cough syrup and pastilles, his throat is choked. It takes a week or ten days to get rid of his ailments.

During these days, he is unable to step out of his flat or even talk to anyone on the phone. The lump in his throat is the size of a golf ball and hurts whenever he opens his mouth. He croaks to his servant and sits in his chair, wrapped in misery. His doctor, who has a clinic in the neighbouring block, is informed that Boota is down with a bad cold and sore throat. Half an hour later, the doctor arrives, wearing a white mask to cover his nose and mouth. He takes Boota's pulse, puts his stethoscope on his chest and back, takes his blood pressure, blood sample, and asks if his bowels have moved. Boota shakes his head.

'Have you phlegm? What colour is it?' he asks.

'Pale.'

The doctor takes out his pad and scribbles names of pills Boota has to take three times a day. That is routine: every visit entails an additional pill or two. Boota is tired of taking pills, two and a half first thing in the morning, eight with breakfast and nine before switching off for the night. Total nineteen, plus three to make it twenty-two and a half. The doctor assures him: 'These pills are not medicines; they are meant to improve your health. At your age you must not take any risks. If your phlegm turns yellow, you must send for me at once. I don't want you to get pneumonia. You may have to be hospitalized. Just take these pills three times a day, and by the grace of Wahguru you will be all right in a couple of days.' He always invokes Wahguru's help when prescribing pills.

The very idea of being in hospital frightens Boota. He'd rather die than have to shit in a bedpan and have his bottom wiped by a nurse. The next time the doctor mentions hospital he'll send his servant to get a capsule of cyanide from the chemist.

For two evenings Boota is missing from the Sunset Club. Baig asks Sharma, 'Panditji, what's wrong with Boota Singh? It's not much fun without him. You live near him. Why not find out?'

'I rang his number this morning, but no one picked up the phone. I will drop in on him on my way home,' replies Sharma.

So he does. He goes through the servants' entrance at the rear with Dabboo Three trailing behind him. He sees

Boota slouched in his chair with a handkerchief pressed to his nose. A glass of rum mixed with hot water, lemon juice and honey is on the table beside him.

'Oy *buddhey*, what's the matter with you?'

Boota shakes his head, points to his throat and croaks: 'Throat, cold, cough.'

'Send for the doctor,' advises Sharma.

'Have,' replies Boota.

'Baig was enquiring after you. I'll tell him,' says Sharma.

Sharma beats a hasty retreat. Boota may be an old friend, but that's no reason to expose himself to catching a cold.

∾

By the time he staggers to his bed, Boota is very drunk. He is not used to drinking rum. And three large helpings laced with honey are more than he can cope with. He recalls Ghalib's lines on *balghami mizaj*:

> Drink as much as you can lay your hands on
> It is the best for anyone with phlegmatic disposition

His nose is blocked, his mouth wide open, as he tries to recall the last time he had as vicious an attack of cold and cough as this one. It was more than forty years ago. He was staying in a small cottage an hour's drive from Paris.

He was desperately trying to write a novel. The widow who owned the cottage worked in his office in Paris and only came to the cottage on weekends, to see her ninety-year-old mother. She had taken on a young German as an au pair to feed her mother and empty her bedpan. She had a part-time gardener to mow the lawn and look after her apple and pear trees. The German girl had a room next to the old woman. Boota was on the ground floor and had the lady's terrier bitch as a companion.

He got on very well with the German girl, a few inches taller than him, golden blonde hair, blue eyes and a full bosom. After she had helped the old woman with her toilet, given her breakfast and put her back in bed, she would come and sit with him in the garden where he sat working on his novel with the terrier bitch sitting near his chair. She could speak English and French fluently. The gardener had a crush on her and began to resent her paying attention to the weird-looking Oriental with a beard on his chin and a turban on his head.

Then Boota went down with a cold. That was a good excuse for the German girl to visit him in his bedroom to enquire about his health. On the third day, his running nose became a clogged nose. He coughed all day and night and spat out phlegm. On the fourth day, when the German girl came to see him, she kissed him on his lips. 'You poor thing! I hope you feel a little better,' she said.

Boota warned her against catching his cold. 'I don't care,' she said. 'I never catch colds.' Later, she brought their dinner to his room and they ate together. At night she came again to bid him: *'Guten nacht—schlafen sie wohl!'*

Having bidden him a good night's sleep, she lay beside him in his bed. They had sex. The next morning, Boota was rid of his cough and cold. The German girl was sneezing.

∾

The following evening Sharma tells Baig: 'Boota is always catching colds. The fellow drinks too much—whisky, rum, vodka, gin, feni, anything. And suffers from chronic constipation. That's asking for trouble, isn't it?'

Baig is more sympathetic. 'Both constipation and cold are controllable. We have some good Yunani herbal medicines for them. I'll send them to him through the servant.'

Back home, Baig tells his Begum about Boota's problem. 'It's not much fun without him. Sharma is too serious; Boota livens up things. I'll send some Yunani medicine to him.'

'I will have some yakhni soup and kwargandal halwa made. Both very good for cold and other problems,' says Begum Baig.

Next morning Baig's servant delivers the medicines, the broth and the halwa at Boota's flat and tells him what time he is to take them. Boota asks the servant to convey his thanks to his master and mistress.

Boota adds Baig's medicine, broth and halwa to his daily intake of food and liquor. On the sixth day the worst is over. He can breathe easily, clears his bowels twice a day and feels the whisky going down his entrails to his belly. And knows all is well with him. He is not sure who to thank: his doctor for giving him twenty-two and a half pills and Wahguru, or Baig and his wife. Maybe none of them. The cold has run its course and will no doubt return when the season changes.

9

SUMMER MERGES
WITH AUTUMN

The Sunset Club does not meet in the first days of September for the simple reason that the rains due in August decided to come a month later. There are intermittent showers for the first four days, and after a break of two days it thunders, but does not rain. A week later, there is a heavy downpour for two days, followed by a day of light drizzle. The daily schedule of the three friends has to change. Sharma spends longer hours at the India International Centre. His mornings are in the library, rummaging through the pages of newspapers and magazines. He has a coffee break, long chit-chats with friends till noon. He has a light south Indian meal and is back home for his siesta.

Boota drives out to take a look at flowers, trees, birds and the Yamuna. The madhumalti creeper on his outer walls is in full bloom. Flowers have begun to appear on the chorisia tree on the lawn facing his flat. The lawn is either under water or dew-washed. He drives to Nigambodh Ghat cremation ground on the right bank of the Yamuna. Three pyres are lit under tin-roofed sheds, with relatives and friends clustered round. The Yamuna is in spate with the waters of melted snows and monsoon rains. Boota spends a good half-hour gazing at the turbulent waters before he returns home in time for a glass of beer and an egg sandwich.

The change in schedule in Baig's household is more radical. Ramadan, the month of fasting and feasting which began in August, continues for another three weeks in September. The Begum Sahiba and the servants are up well before dawn to prepare for the morning meal which has to be eaten before sunrise. Adults eat and drink nothing till sunset. Children are exempted from the ordeal. So is the Nawab Sahib. Others gorge themselves in the morning, to be able to fast all day. Baig gets up at his usual hour, has his tea and cigar, lunch and whisky and dinner. Year after year he repeats Ghalib's words: When the poet was asked how many days did he not observe the fast, he replied, 'Not one single day.' It could mean he had fasted all the month or not fasted for a single day. He laughs when he repeats the joke. Everyone laughs as if they were hearing it for the first time.

♫

Sharma can't help having a dig at Baig. 'Baig, all this business of stuffing yourself before dawn, doing nothing all day and once again stuffing yourself after sunset, is not the way to fast. It is bad for your health. We Hindus have a more sensible way of fasting: we omit the kinds of food which are your daily diet and drink as much water as we can—it flushes the system. Don't you agree?'

'You may be right. That's why I take Ramadan as I take other months of the year,' replies Baig.

Boota sounds a triumphant note. 'Both Hindus and Muslims are on the wrong track. We Sikhs don't believe in fasting, only feasting.'

They laugh. Sharma resumes: 'And this business of Iftaar parties. Most Hindu and Sikh politicians throw Iftaar parties, invite a few Muslim celebrities to join them. Also journalists, so they can get political mileage out of the exercise. Thoroughly dishonest, don't you think?'

'I agree,' says Baig. 'I am often invited. I never go.'

♫

Unseasonal rains take their toll of life. On the second day of the month, a helicopter carrying the chief minister of Andhra Pradesh crashes into a dense jungle, killing all its occupants. Boota reads about the incident on the front pages of all the national dailies he gets. Though well informed, he is unaware that the late chief minister and his family were Christians. Sharma reads about it in the India International Centre library and asks his friends, 'Did you know Reddy was Christian?' Baig's Begum reads out the news to her husband and comments: 'Once upon a time the state was the kingdom of the Nizams of Hyderabad. It had Muslim rulers and aristocracy—Jangs, Jahs, Dowlahs. They all spoke Urdu. Then Hindus took it over and made it Telugu-speaking Andhra. Then came the turn of *Isaees* to rule. Janoo, did you know the chief minister was a Christian?'

'Was he?' asks Baig. 'There could not be many Christians in the state. How the world changes!'

'Not much. Reddy's son has announced his succession to the throne and a majority of members of the Assembly have promised support. They are sure Sonia Gandhi, who is the real ruler of the country, being Christian, will undoubtedly back him. That is the way of the world,' says the Begum.

'Wait and see.'

ॐ

The weather continues to be a spoilsport. If it does not rain, it threatens to rain. On the 10th, 11th and 12th it rains intermittently all day and night. It is only on the 15th that the sun comes out and soaks up the moisture on the ground and in the air. By then, Andhra Pradesh is old news. Sonia Gandhi put her foot down on the upstart son of the late chief minister and his opportunist supporters and ordered the Hindu Rosaiah to be acting chief minister. The big news was the death two days earlier of Norman Borlaug, winner of the Nobel Prize and father of the Green Revolution. He was ninety-five.

Baig's Begum did not tell her husband about it as the name meant nothing to her. For Sharma and Boota it provides another opportunity to show off what they know about the Green Revolution.

'Long time no see,' says Boota when the three meet after a couple of weeks.

'What kind of English is this?' asks Sharma.

'The latest, spoken by the young generation of today. Keep up with the times. Anyhow, you must have read of the death of Norman Borlaug?'

'One of the greatest of men who trod on the face of the earth,' says Sharma in a pontifical tone. 'By his name I thought he was some kind of Scandinavian. He turns out to be American.'

Baig feels left out of the dialogue and protests. 'Bhai, please tell me who this Borlaug Sahib was? My Begum told me nothing about him.'

'One of the greatest men who trod the face of the earth,' repeats Sharma, pointing his finger to the sky.

Boota enlightens Baig. 'Mian Sahib, if there was no Borlaug most of us would have starved to death. You ask me why and I will tell you—we had run out of wheat stocks. Both we and Pakistan were living on American charity. Then Borlaug, having experimented with a new variety of short wheat in Mexico, which was rust-resistant, arrived in India in 1963 with samples of his new crop. He trained our fellows in the Ludhiana Agricultural University and advised them to get out of their laboratories, go to the farms and teach farmers how to grow the Mexican wheat. He did the same in Pakistan. In ten years both countries were able to become self-sufficient in food because he also evolved new varieties of rice and maize. That is what we call the Green Revolution. It was a miracle. He was a miracle man, the Vishnu avatar of our times.'

'May his soul rest in peace,' says Baig. 'I will tell my Begum about him. But if we go on breeding recklessly, as we are, we will again be going round from door to door with our begging bowls.'

By the last week of September the monsoon disappears but there is a nip in the air morning and evening. It presages the onset of autumn and cooler days to come. Kalidas, who was a keener observer of nature than other ancient poets, described the onset of autumn lyrically:

The autumn comes, a maiden fair
In slenderness and grace,
With nodding rice-stems in her hair,
And lilies in her face
In flowers of grasses she is clad
And as she moves along,
Birds greet her with their cooing glad
Like bracelets' tinkling song.

Kalidas also wrote about the post-monsoon period as the beginning of the season of fulfilment:

Over the rice-fields, laden plants
Are shivering to the breeze;
While in his brisk caresses dance
The blossom-burdened trees;
He ruffles every lily-pond
Where blossoms kiss and part,
And stirs with lover's fancies fond
The young man's eager heart.

A significant step against encroachments made by different religious communities on public land was taken when this practice was roundly criticized by the Supreme Court. Like many of its other pronouncements, it was another pious platitude, of which no one was going to take any notice. Hindus and Sikhs would continue to take out huge processions through bazaars and force shops to close down. Muslims would continue to block roads to offer namaaz on their auspicious days. Peepal tree boles would continue to be smeared with red and shrines go up round them. Mountain tops would continue to have temples built on them, myths spread about their origin, and about miracles that happened there, and can happen again so that priests and preachers of religion can fill their bellies and feel good.

The members of the Sunset Club have different views on the subject: 'Do what you like but with moderation,' says Baig.

'Why should it become such an important issue that the Supreme Court has to pronounce on it? It is for the administration to decide limits of encroachment,' says Boota. 'I would put a blanket ban on misuse of public places for religious purposes, but people have great respect for bogus religiosity.'

10

GANDHI'S OCTOBER

The two nicest months to be in Delhi are February and October. In February the winter chill loosens its grip, the sky is a clear blue, it is cool and soothing. And signs of spring are in the air. It is the other way round in October. The summer's heat and the dampness caused by monsoon rains evaporate. The skies are a cloudless blue, the sun no longer scorches and pleasant autumn breezes blow. Consequently, there are more people to be seen in Lodhi Gardens during these two months than at other times of the year.

If you happen to be in the garden during these months, sitting on the Boorha Binch, fix your gaze skywards. You may see a bewitching spectacle connected with the change of seasons. In February you will see a wavering V-shaped flight of geese, or maybe ducks, calling each other, flying from east to west, from India towards the Himalayas, to their summer abodes in Central Asia. In October you will see the same band of wavering V-shaped flights of geese or ducks calling to each other, flying from west to east, from Central Asia to the wetlands, rivers and lakes of India. You may even spot a lone cuckoo calling *kooh-ku, kooh-ku*, as it flies overhead, making its way to the hills for the summer months, and in October flying back to spend its winter in the plains of India.

While the weather in Delhi during these two months is predictable, it is not so in other parts of the country. October 2009 begins with heavy rains and rivers in spate in Andhra Pradesh and Karnataka. Even in Delhi there was a mild drizzle on the 6th and the sky was clouded the next day which was Karva Chauth, the day when Hindu and Sikh women observe a day's fast for the health and longevity of their husbands. It meant nothing to members of the Sunset Club: Sharma is a bachelor, Boota a widower and Baig a Muslim.

The 2nd of October, being Gandhi's birthday, is a gazetted holiday. Political leaders once again make their way to the Gandhi Samadhi at Rajghat, to be photographed strewing flowers on the slab of black marble marking the site of his cremation. Most people listen to his favourite soul-stirring hymns: 'Know him as the man of God who feels another's pain,' and 'Ishwar and Allah are thy names, may the Almighty bless us all.' Then they go to the gardens and parks for a day's picnic. Lodhi Gardens is the most favoured spot for those who live near it.

The Sunset Club meets as usual a couple of hours before the sun goes down. Baig opens the dialogue by remarking, 'Lots of raunaq today.'

Sharma explains, 'It is Gandhi Jayanti. All offices and shops are closed in his memory. He was the greatest of the great who trod the face of the earth.'

'You said the same words about Norman Borlaug,' Boota points out.

Sharma hates being snubbed, especially by Boota. He retorts, 'Both great men in their own ways; one catered to the body, the other to the soul.'

'Whatever that means,' says Boota scornfully.

Baig intervenes to restore peace. 'You will agree that he was the prophet of modern India. Not only did he get us independence from the British, he won respect for India all over the world. All through preaching love and renouncing hate.'

'He was murdered by an Indian Brahmin, a *jaat bhai* of Sharmaji. He could not have killed Gandhi if he had not hated him,' says Boota.

As expected, Sharma is provoked to retaliate. 'Why bring caste into a criminal act?' he asks. 'Many great people were murdered by mad men—Abraham Lincoln, Kennedy; and Indira Gandhi was killed by Boota's jaat bhais, her own Sikh bodyguards.'

To stop his friends wrangling with each other, Baig has to intervene again. 'Forget those unimportant details. You will agree that Gandhi profoundly influenced the lives of all Indians. And to the world outside, India is known as the land of Gandhi. He should be our role model. We should try to follow his example, shouldn't we?'

'No one does,' retorts Boota. 'He was for prohibition and had it included in our Constitution. If he had had his way, none of us would be enjoying our evening drinks. Now there is no prohibition in India except in his home state, Gujarat. And Gujjoos have liquor flowing like the river Sabarmati. And more die from drinking spurious hooch there than anywhere else in India. For that matter, he was also a vegetarian and regarded killing animals for food a sin. Yet all three of us are meat eaters.'

Sharma corrects him, 'Actually, four things were not allowed in his ashram—no meat, no alcohol, no tobacco and no sex.'

'Our friend Boota disagrees with everything we say,' says Baig. 'Is there anything else you find wrong about Gandhi?'

'I do. His views on sex. Without as much as consulting his wife, he took a vow of celibacy. Then he fought a lifelong battle to control his libido. He had women to massage him. He had young girls sleep stark naked on the floor on either side of him, gave enemas to them, bathed naked with them, just to make sure he did not get dirty thoughts and erections. Then he had wet dreams and told everyone about them. All three of us have had sex in our younger days. No regrets. If we could, we would have it today, wouldn't we?'

'Speak for yourself,' replies Sharma. 'I am content to attain *brahmacharya*.'

'But I am sure you have sex on your mind. Don't deny it,' says Boota.

'Arrey bhai, sex is on everyone's mind,' adds Baig. 'Some more, some less, but it is there.'

'I have a theory about it,' says Boota. 'If you would like to hear about it, I will be happy to spell it out for you. But you may not approve of the vocabulary I have to use.'

'Go ahead,' says Sharma. 'Nothing you say shocks us any more.'

Boota spells out his theory. 'It is like this. Sex is the most potent force in our lives and governs most of our actions. In the case of males, it is centred on the appendage in his middle. It goes through four stages of development, all beginning with the letter L. First it is a *lullee*, the size of one's little finger. A male child is hardly aware of it besides it being the conduit of his pee-pee, soo-soo. Only his ayah or maidservants, if any, play with it when bathing him. By the age of five it becomes a *lull* and begins to get erections. Boys of that age try to find other boys or girls to stick it into their bottoms. Nothing comes out of it. The third stage is reached around twelve or thirteen when it becomes a *lulla* or laura or *lund*. Curly hair begins to sprout round its base and the urge to stick it in a male's bottom or a female's middle becomes irrepressible—it may be a friend, boy-servant, maidservant, cousin or aunt. If none is available, he takes matters in hand and masturbates and wastes his seed in the air. Then he gets himself a wife and goes into her as often as he can till she becomes pregnant. Then he looks out for other women available to him, and so it goes on into the seventies and early eighties. The fourth and last stage it becomes a limpoo. Then it rarely gets a full erection—only a half-hearted raising of its head—and is waxen-soft. All sex which found expression through it moves to his head. But it never leaves the male till the last day of his life. Does this make sense to you?'

'You should write a thesis on the subject,' says Sharma. 'Perhaps some university may confer a Doctorate of Lullology on you.'

'Boota Singhji, I am on your side. I agree with your analysis of male behaviour. But how will I be able to tell my Begum about it? She always asks me what we talked about.'

'Tell her we discussed the Gandhian legacy,' suggests Sharma.

Boota changes his tune and says, 'I'll tell you why I respect Gandhi despite all his eccentricities. He never told a lie. He was a living example of Nanak's exhortation:

Truth above all
Above truth
Truthful conduct

'He translated this into a practical code of living. So he forged his powerful weapons, satyagraha and ahimsa, to fight the strong. And he won his battle without firing a shot.'

Even Sharma is impressed. 'It is like the devil quoting the scriptures,' he says. 'Bhai Boota, this is the first time I have heard you talk sense.'

Baig concedes, 'Now I can give my Begum a learned discourse on why Gandhi was great. Thanks, Bootaji.'

Boota acknowledges the compliments by salaaming both his friends in Muslim style.

On that happy note they part for the day.

ॐ

However, the topic comes up again in the homes of Sharma and Baig.

Sharma's sister asks him what they talked about in the park. He tells her in one word: 'Gandhi.'

'Gandhi! How boring! What is there to say about Gandhi which has not been said a thousand times before? And all that remains of him are bhajans at his birth and death anniversaries.'

'To the outside world India is known as the land of Gandhi,' repeats Sharma.

'Sheh!' she scoffs. 'In the land of Gandhi no one follows his teachings.' She goes back to watch TV with the servants' children.

Baig's Begum asks her husband the same question and gets the same one-word answer: 'Gandhi.'

'Nothing remains of Gandhi anywhere in the world, except his name,' she says. 'Look at all the violence in our own country. Marxists, Naxalites killing policemen in tribal areas. Hindus killing Muslims in his home state of Gujarat, now ruled over by that anti-Muslim chief minister, Narendra Modi. In Pakistan, bombs exploding in Peshawar, Kohat, Lahore; Sunnis killing Shias. In Afghanistan, Muslims killing each other by the dozen. And in Yemen, Iraq, Iran—everywhere. Gandhi has become a legend. Now all that Gandhi means is good intentions without the desire to practise them.'

Baig interrupts her harangue: 'Achha, achha, Begum. Now let me enjoy my whisky in peace.'

'We Indians have a genius for making beautiful things as ugly as possible,' Boota tells Baig on the evening of the 17th of October. Sharma is missing.

'What is bothering you now?' asks Baig.

'Here we have Diwali, the most important and beautiful festival of India. And what have we done to it?' asks Boota.

'I had forgotten it is Diwali today. Sharmaji must be busy entertaining his relatives this evening,' says Baig.

'How can you forget it?' asks Boota. 'They start reminding you of its advent a week before by bursting crackers. I have to use earplugs to prevent explosions bursting my eardrums. Tonight it will sound like a full-scale war with cannons booming, bombs exploding till after midnight.'

'Don't you Sikhs also celebrate Diwali?' asks Baig.

'We celebrate every Hindu festival and with even more noise,' replies Boota. 'My daughter is married to a Hindu. She and her daughter light candles and oil lamps in their apartment and mine. I just step in to see the lights. I can tell which flat is Hindu or Sikh because they have rows of candles on their windows. Those that don't have them are occupied by Muslims or Christians. Or there has been a death in the family. It is as simple as that.'

'We don't have many bombs exploding in our locality; all our neighbours are educated. They light candles only, let off sparklers. Even my Begum keeps a few *diyas* on the gates so that we don't appear different,' says Baig.

'Sharma gives some money to his servants so they can have fun. He eats a lot of sweets and gets gas in his stomach. Eating and gambling is compulsory on Diwali. Much like your Eid-ul-Fitr, except you don't gamble or let off crackers!' says Boota.

'Bootaji, you are in a bad mood this evening. Cheer up. Diwali mubarak,' says Baig.

I I

THE GURU'S NOVEMBER

Fifteen days after Diwali, which lights up a moonless night, comes the most important day in the Sikh calendar—the birth anniversary of the founder Guru Nanak (1469–1539), on the night of the full moon. By then it has become distinctly cooler and people start wearing shawls or sweaters, days become shorter as evening shadows begin to lengthen soon after 5 p.m. There are not many flowering trees to be seen besides chorisias and cassias; and in the gardens of the rich, chrysanthemums of different colours.

Let us return to the Guru. Begum Baig has instructed her husband to be sure to give *mubarakbaad* to Boota on his Guru's birth anniversary. So, no sooner than he meets Boota, he says, '*Guruji ka janamdin mubarak ho.*'

Sharma butts in, 'Baig Sahib, the proper way is to say it in Punjabi: *"Gurpurb dee lakh lakh vadhaaee hovey,"* which means hundred thousand, hundred thousand congratulations on the Guru's birthday.'

Baig repeats the words as best he can.

'Thanks,' replies Boota, 'but I don't even go to a gurdwara.'

'He is a cunning Sardar,' says Sharma. 'He writes about Sikhs and their religion and receives honours from them and at the same time pretends to be an agnostic and rationalist. He wins both ways.'

Before it becomes a slanging match, Baig intervenes. 'I confess my ignorance. I know very little about Sikhism besides Sikhs being monotheist, against idol worship. Like Muslims, they are *ahil-e-kitaab*—people of the Book—and they don't believe in caste. They are known to be a warrior race.'

Sharma is in an aggressive mood. 'Let me put the record straight. Everything in Sikhism is taken from Hinduism. Its theology is based on the Upanishads but written in Punjabi. Yes, Sikhs are monotheists; so are many Hindus. Sikhs are against idol worship, but they treat their holy book like an idol. They drape it in expensive silks, wake it up in the morning—*prakash*—and put it to sleep in the evening—*santokh*. On special days they take it out in huge processions as Hindus take out their gods and goddesses. As for being a casteless community, the less said the better. All Indian communities have their own caste systems, be they Hindus, Muslims, Christians or Sikhs. It is fashionable to put the blame on Hindu Brahmins. Sikhs have three castes—Jats who are in the majority; non-Jats comprising Khatris and Vaishyas; and the outcaste Mazhabis. They don't intermarry. Not one of the Sikhs' ten Gurus married outside the Khatri caste. Mazhabis continue to be treated as untouchables—in many villages they have separate gurdwaras, so their claim of being casteless is a lot of bakwaas or bullshit as Boota would put it.'

'But Mazhabis have access to all gurdwaras and join other castes in eating in *guru ka langar*,' protests Boota. 'It is not as bad as in the case of Hindus who neither want to let them in many of their temples nor share the same food.'

'Agreed,' concedes Sharma. 'It is the difference between nineteen and twenty—*unnis–bees ka farak*. And as to being a warrior race which they boast about so much, so are the Rajputs, Marathas, Gorkhas—all Hindus. Muslims have Pathans. This warrior business is not something to boast about—it has no substance.'

Baig tries to diffuse the situation. 'Sharmaji, you want me to take back the lakh-lakh congratulations from Boota Singh?'

'Sounds like that, doesn't it?' says Boota. 'You utter a sentence of criticism against Hinduism and they are up in arms. For them Hinduism is always in danger of being polluted.'

Sharma launches into a sermon. 'Hinduism is the only religion in the world which is not based on the teachings of a prophet but on eternal truths spelt out in the Vedas, the Upanishads and the Gita. Religions born out of Hinduism, like Jainism, Buddhism and Sikhism, were all prophet based and emphasized some aspect or other of the mother religion. But Sikhs hate to admit that the teachings in their sacred scripture, the Adi Granth, are entirely based on Hinduism. Even its names for God are Hindu, like Hari, Ram, Govind, Vitthal and a dozen others, with only one name of its own coinage—Wahguru, which was coined by their bards.'

Before Boota can get a word in, Sharma continues his sermon, this time directing his words to Baig. 'All Western religions are prophet based—Zoroastrianism on Zarathustra, Judaism on the Old Testament prophets, Christianity on Jesus Christ, Islam on Prophet Mohammad and the Koran revealed to him by Allah's messenger. Most of its practices are borrowed from Judaism. To pray, Jews turn to Jerusalem and go on pilgrimage there. Muslims turn to Makka and Madina and go there on Haj or Umra. The names of all their prayers are borrowed from the Jews. Jews bleed the animals and birds they eat and call it kosher. Muslims do the same and call it halal.

Jews consider pigs unclean and do not eat pork or bacon. Muslims also consider the pig unclean and believe its meat is haram—forbidden. Jews circumcise male children; so do Muslims and call it *sunnat*—tradition.'

Baig and Boota listen to Sharma's sermon to the end. Baig is evidently upset but tries not to show it. 'Panditji, if I may be permitted to ask you two questions. I would like to know, if Hinduism is the first and the greatest of all religions, why do more people subscribe to Christianity or Islam? And secondly, why is Islam today actually said to be the fastest growing religion?'

Before Sharma can reply, Boota butts in: 'And allow me to add one more question to Baig's. If all you say is true, why are Hindus more ridden with superstition than any other people? Why is the Ganga holy? Like other rivers it is made of melted snow and rain. Why is a dip in its dirty waters regarded as holy, to cleanse the body and the soul? Its waters, which get dirtier and dirtier as it flows along, soil the body. And as for the soul, no one knows about it . . .'

Sharma does not deign to respond. He feels he has made his point, and that as his friends ponder over what he has said, they will concede he is right. He decides to return home early to celebrate his victory over Boota with an extra drink.

Boota feels a bit frustrated having Sharma score over him. There is still light; November sunshine can be luminous. A clear blue sky lights up with a silvery hue as the sun goes down. Boota decides to take a round of Sikandar Lodhi's tomb before returning home. He bids Baig 'Khuda Hafiz' and slowly walks down the slope to the moat bridge and up towards the western wall of Sikandar Lodhi's tomb. There used to be holes in the wall where spotted owlets could be seen taking in the sun with their eyes shut. If anyone stopped to look at them, they sensed it and opened their eyes, then bobbed their heads up and down before withdrawing into their holes. The wall had come down and was rebuilt without holes. This evening, a couple of owlets are sitting on the parapet, and Boota stops to gaze at them. They make their usual menacing gestures before flying off to the rear side of the tomb. Boota recalls Sudraka's lines:

> *Slowly the darkness drains away the sunlight.*
> *Drawn homewards to their nests, the crows fall silent.*
> *And now the owl sits on the hollow tree,*
> *Bolder, neck sunk inside his body,*
> *And stares; swivels his head; and stares.*

He goes round the tomb walls. On the northern side are a few saptaparni (seven-leafed) trees. He can't see any flowers but catches their cinnamon-scented fragrance as he goes past, walking towards his car. He resolves to settle scores with Sharma as soon as he can.

Baig is left alone. His servant puts a shawl round his shoulders and reminds him, 'Sahib, your friends have left; we should get back. It is getting chilly.'

Baig gets up reluctantly and is pushed in his wheelchair to his car. His Begum greets him with a broad smile. 'You are early this evening. Didn't your friends turn up?'

'They did. And for once Sharma got the better of Boota Singh.'

'About what?'

'Well, I congratulated Boota for Guru Nanak's birth anniversary. Before Boota could say anything, Sharma delivered a lecture on how everything in Sikhism was borrowed from Hinduism and they are as caste-ridden as other communities. And that sort of thing.'

'There is some truth in what Sharma says. All of us have caste differences of our own. There was our holy Prophet Hazrat Mohammad—peace be upon Him—who told us we were all equals and chose a *Habshi*, a Negro, Hazrat Bilal, to be our first muezzin. And look at us now. Allama Iqbal wrote about Sultan Mahmud and his slave Ayyaz standing shoulder to shoulder when offering namaaz in the mosque. But no sooner were they finished than Mahmud became the Sultan and Ayyaz his slave. We are told that Islam means peace and acceptance of God's will. And look at Muslims now. Every day you hear of bombs blowing up mosques in Pakistan, Mussalmans killing

Mussalmans in Iraq, Iran and Afghanistan. What's left of true Islam, you tell me?'

'Achha, achha, Begum, I have heard you repeat this again and again. Don't ruin the taste of my whisky.'

'Also forbidden by the Koran. You are a *naklee* Mussalman.'

'*Ameen.* So be it.'

∾

Two days later Gandhi's name again becomes the topic of debate at the Sunset Club. And for a totally different but valid reason. Madhu Koda, chief minister of Jharkhand, is charged with corruption on a massive scale. He comes from a poor family of small farmers. Within a month of taking up office, he becomes a multi-billionaire by mortgaging the assets of the state he rules. His predecessor and successor, Shibu Soren, had also been charged with moneymaking and murder.

'That's what remains of Gandhi,' says Sharma. 'Men like Soren and Koda pay homage to Gandhi twice a year and spend the other 363 days stealing public money.'

'How can you blame Gandhi for the rampant corruption in our society?' asks Boota.

'I am not blaming him,' replies Sharma. 'All I am saying is that he has become irrelevant.'

'I can tell you that no one who makes money by illicit means can be at peace with himself,' says Baig. '*Haram ka paisa hazam nahin hota*—you cannot digest money earned by cheating others.'

'Baig, that is a myth,' says Boota. '*Khoob hazam hota hai*—it is most digestible. If you have lots of money, no matter where it comes from, you can enjoy the best of food, live in comfort, enjoy holidays in the hills during summer and get the best of doctors and medicines when you fall ill. And if, unfortunately, you are caught taking a bribe, you can get away by giving bigger bribes. You might have noticed that the corrupt do not die young. They manage to cross eighty.'

'Like the three of us,' adds Sharma with a broad smile, 'that is, assuming that none of us is corrupt!'

Begum Baig has more to say about corruption after she hears what her husband and his friends had to say on the subject. 'You say that nothing disturbs the sleep of the corrupt, but you don't say why they snore peacefully through the night. I'll tell you why. Because they have no *zameer*—conscience. Only those who have a conscience feel guilty when they have done something wrong.'

'True,' adds Baig. 'I suppose it is the same with pickpockets, thieves, robbers and murderers. They have no sense of shame. So they never suffer from pangs of guilt.'

'Allah be thanked, no one in our family has wrongfully deprived another of his property,' says Begum Sahiba. 'That is why Allah has been good to us.'

'That is the reason why I approve of Gandhi's teachings,' says Baig. 'Don't hurt anyone and you will be rewarded. I know I am not a good Mussalman but I have never done anyone any harm. I only want to enjoy life as long as I can, a bit like Emperor Babur, who said, "Enjoy life to the full because you have only one life to live: *Babur ba aish kosh, kay zindagi do baara n'est.*"'

Autumn rapidly gives way to winter. On the 11th there is a drizzle which brings the temperature down by a few degrees. A week later chilly winds blow across the city. People wear woollen caps, mufflers, sweaters during the day. After sunset they wrap themselves in quilts. The well-to-do have log fires, watch TV. There is a Doordarshan programme on happenings in Pakistan—bombs exploding in Peshawar, Kohat, Rawalpindi and Lahore. And they thank their lucky stars they are living in India.

I2

DECEMBER OF THE
BLUE MOON

So we come to the last month of the year 2009.

Most mornings begin with mist, fog or smog. The temperature begins to drop rapidly as snow falls on the Himalayas, barely a hundred miles away as the crow flies. The only flowers in bloom are chrysanthemums, marigolds and roses. It is a good month for the young who can enjoy the bracing cold breeze because their blood is warm. It is a sad month for the old because their blood is cold; they catch colds, get sore throats and respiratory problems, cough with phlegm. Many get pneumonia and pass away. More old people die in December and January than in other months of the year.

On the 1st of December, Baig is the last to arrive in Lodhi Gardens, and he is in a bad temper. 'It took me an hour to get here,' he says. 'Traffic was held up by the police because Sonia Gandhi and the prime minister had to go to the Electric Crematorium. Some big shot must have died this morning. My Begum told me nothing about it.'

'It was S.K. Singh, governor of Rajasthan,' Boota tells him. 'Good, honest and able fellow, and not too old. But that is no excuse to block all traffic. Anyway, did you read about the four generals being named for making illicit money on the sale of public land? They draw high salaries, live in rent-free bungalows, eat free in the Officers' Mess, enjoy free medical treatment and medicines and draw handsome pensions. That is not enough for some buggers so they make money on the side. And when caught, bring disgrace to the armed forces.'

'My Begum did not tell me about them either,' says Baig.

❧

In the middle of the month Boota Singh goes down with yet another cold. It is the sixth time in the year. He has done nothing wrong to bring it on. On the contrary, he has been regularly chewing Haliborange tablets, sipping Limsip, gargling with Listerine. Every time it reoccurs, it is worse than the last. It must be in his genes; he thinks he is meant to die of pneumonia.

For three days and nights his nose is blocked; every time he coughs, he brings up phlegm. And he coughs incessantly. Sharma hears about it from Boota's servant and advises him to tell his master to consult his doctor: '*Us gadhey ko kaho daktar bulaye.*'

Baig hears about it from Sharma and says: 'He is always going down with colds; doesn't look after himself.'

The afternoons on the Boorha Binch become shorter and more formal; both Baig and Sharma return to their homes well before sunset.

Begum Baig is surprised at her husband's returning early from Lodhi Gardens. Baig explains: 'It is not much fun when Boota is not there. Sharma has little to say unless he is provoked.'

'*Bechaara*—poor fellow,' says Begum. 'I will send him some yakhni.'

After six days, there is a drizzle. The temperature drops by a couple of degrees. Boota fears his cold and cough will get worse. Exactly the opposite happens: his nose clears, he stops coughing. He is eager to exchange views with his friends.

The drizzle does not last long. The sky is a clear blue. The sun lightens up the world. Boota reads the report of the Liberhan Commission on the destruction of the Babri

Masjid, seventeen years after the event and at a cost of over seven crore rupees. That should be enough for a lively debate.

Boota turns up at the Sunset Club looking very cheerful. Sharma is also in high spirits and says: 'O buddhey, what happens to you every fourth day?'

'Bhai, this time I really thought my end had come; I told my servant if anything happens to me, divide my stock of liquor equally—send half to Sharma, half to Baig.' He quotes an Urdu couplet:

No one knows when his death is due.
He hoards for a hundred years,
Of his tomorrow he has no clue.

'Wah, wah! exclaims Baig. 'So you still have enough to last you a century.'

They have a good laugh. Baig brings up the Liberhan findings. Sharma remarks: 'Whenever our government is in trouble, it appoints a commission. Commissions take their own sweet time. Good salaries, free house, free travel, etc., etc., for the members. By the time they hand over their reports, people have forgotten what it was all about. Remember the commissions to find out whether or not Netaji Subhas Chandra Bose had really been killed in an air crash or was still alive? And the half a dozen commissions on the anti-Sikh riots of 1984? There must be dozens of others gathering dust in the archives.'

'Surely this one is a more scandalous waste of money than any commission before it,' says Boota. 'We saw the whole drama enacted on TV: BJP netas sitting on the dais watching the tamasha. Shiv Sena goondas mounting the dome of the mosque with axes, spades, etc., and knocking it down. It must have been known to that Kalyan Singh, chief minister of Uttar Pradesh, and that spineless prime minister, Narasimha Rao. We saw Uma Bharati hug Murli Manohar Joshi when the task was done. No one tried to stop the shameless bastards from knocking down a place of worship. Advani, who started the whole mischief, became the most powerful minister in the BJP government. He now calls it the saddest day of his life. He has never apologized for doing what he did. A senior IPS officer, Anju Gupta, who was assistant superintendent of police, Ayodhya, during the demolition period, and was assigned as Advani's personal security officer, has deposed before the special CBI court, saying the speech made by Advani at Ayodhya shortly before the Babri Masjid was demolished was inflammatory. He repeated many times that the Ram Temple would be constructed at the very site where the mosque stood.'

Boota continues, 'As for that *mukhota*—double-faced— Vajpayee, you never know what goes on in his mind. For him, heads I win, tails you lose.'

Sharma protests mildly, 'I agree breaking the mosque was shameful. But so is breaking of temples. Muslim invaders destroyed hundreds of Hindu temples—the most important being Somnath, which Advani chose to be the starting point of his Rath Yatra. Memories of destroyed temples still rankle in the minds of millions of people. It is human nature.'

'Surely, there must be an end to this tit-for-tat behaviour,' says Boota. 'You break my temple, I break your mosque. We had hoped that with Independence we would put the past behind us. Don't you agree, Baig?'

Baig simply nods his head. He senses that Boota's abusive language for the perpetrators of the foul deed is meant to convince Muslims that there are non-Muslims who share their hurt. He is eager to tell his Begum what Boota said. It will surely please her. But he is non-committal in his reply. 'It is true we embarked on our journey into freedom with high hopes. They have been cruelly belied. So much communal hatred and violence I have not known ever before.'

They sit in silence, pondering over the matter. The sun has gone and it has turned chilly. Baig's servant comes up and pleads with him. 'Sahib, it has become very cold now. Begum Sahiba must be getting worried.'

All three get up reluctantly and bid each other goodbye, 'Till tomorrow.'

Begum Sahiba is indeed somewhat worried. 'You are late. What kept you sitting out in the cold?'

'I'll tell you,' he replies. 'We had a very interesting discussion. But first let me have a sip of my whisky. I am chilled.'

He relaxes in his chair by the fireside. The maidservants begin to press his legs. His manservant brings a bottle of Black Label, soda and ice. Baig pours himself a stiff one. Begum Sahiba puts her dupatta across her nose to express her disapproval, but for a change sits by him and repeats: 'So, what were you talking about this evening?'

'The report on the demolition of the Babri Masjid,' replies Baig. And proceeds to tell her what Sharma and Boota had to say about it. She makes no comment on Sharma's explanation. When Baig ends his narrative, she speaks up loudly: 'Not even Allah will forgive these fellows for what they have done. All these goondas will rot in *jehennum*. You take it from me, anyone who damages a house of prayer deserves the most dire punishment.'

For once even the servants, who have been listening intently, nod their heads. One says loudly, 'Begum Sahiba is absolutely right. These fellows should be flogged in public.'

After a big gulp of whisky, Baig asks, 'And what should have been done to Muslims who demolished Hindu temples?'

No one replies. Not even the Begum Sahiba. They switch on the TV. There is news of bomb blasts in several cities of Pakistan, some in mosques when people were offering namaaz.

∾

As if there is not enough turmoil in the country, major violence erupts in Hyderabad in early December. A politician with a nose like a potato announces a fast unto death unless Andhra Pradesh is split into three parts and a new state of Telangana, which includes Hyderabad, is immediately conceded. As his fast proceeds and he loses weight, his nose gets more spud-like. And riots break out in Hyderabad. Buses are set on fire, shops are closed, students of Osmania University go on a rampage, wrecking furniture. Everyone forgets that the entire concept of dividing India into different states was based on the language spoken in the region. All of Andhra Pradesh is Telugu-speaking, so cutting off Rayalaseema and coastal Andhra is a flagrant departure from the principal of one language, one state. Nevertheless, as Chandrasekhara Rao's health deteriorates and doctors say he won't last long, the government panics and on the 10th of December announces its readiness to concede Telangana. As expected, overnight there are similar demands for separate states in different parts of the country. The government tries the old ruse to play for time—it sets up a committee of experts to examine the pros and cons of a separate Telangana. The turmoil subsides—for a time.

On the 23rd, the results of assembly elections in Jharkhand are announced. No party wins a clear majority. But Shibu Soren, with a criminal past, comes to an understanding with a newly formed BJP, under a new leader. Loudly proclaiming a new political morality, it agrees to lend support to the proven-corrupt Shibu Soren. As the French saying goes, the more it changes the more it is the same thing.

On Christmas Eve, Boota goes over to Sharma's flat to have a quick drink and to find out how he means to celebrate the birth of Jesus Christ. He finds Sharma sitting by the fireside with a stack of Christmas and New Year cards on the table beside him, scribbling addresses of senders of good wishes. Across his sitting room stretch two strings making an X with cards strung on them.

'What are you up to?' asks Boota.

'Look at all these,' answers Sharma, 'cards from all over the world. Feels good to know people still remember you. Help yourself to a drink.'

Boota pours out a whisky for himself and sits down. 'What a waste of money!' he says.

Sharma's sister agrees. 'He must have blown up over one thousand rupees on the cards. And now a couple of thousand more on foreign and domestic postage stamps.'

'Don't you reply to people who wish you joy and happiness?' asks Sharma looking up.

'I don't,' replies Boota. 'I simply toss the greeting cards I receive in the waste-paper basket. They are a meaningless ritual.'

'Each one to his taste,' says Sharma and raises his glass. 'Cheers!'

'Cheers,' replies Boota. He gulps down his whisky. 'Any programme for tomorrow?'

'None,' replies Sharma. 'I'll just clear my Christmas mail and go to Lodhi Gardens in the evening. See you there.'

Boota pats Dabboo Three on the head and says, 'So, happy Christmas. Cheers.'

Boota trudges home. He has a sprig of mistletoe hanging above his entrance door, but no woman to kiss. Christmas Eve is special to him: it reminds him of the many he spent in English homes. He pours himself a single malt with soda and ice and settles down in his chair by the fireside. He switches on his tape recorder which has all his favourite Christmas carols, like 'Silent Night Holy Night', 'The Holly and the Ivy', and a dozen others, ending with a chorus singing 'Auld Lang Syne'. In between, he has a second single malt and recalls scenes of Christmas Eve parties in England. Many a sigh escapes his lips. Why on earth does he love the English so much? He is ashamed of admitting it to his Indian friends. But it is okay admitting it to himself. He shouts to his servant Bahadur to warm up his dinner and open a bottle of Barolo. Bahadur brings his dinner on a tray and puts it beside him. Boota pours the wine in the wine glass. Bahadur waits impatiently to serve him dessert and get back to his quarter. It is well past his sahib's dinnertime. However, the sahib takes his own sweet time, relishing the Christmas pudding laced with brandy that he had specially ordered for the evening. His Christmas Eve dinner is not complete without cognac in a special balloon glass. You can sniff its bouquet before you savour it with your tongue.

By the time he has finished with his meal, he is sozzled and heavy with sleep. He dozes off in his armchair. He is not aware when Bahadur takes his tray away and switches off the extra lights. By the time he wakes up, the fire in the grate has died down and the room has turned chilly. He goes to the bathroom to empty his bladder, keeping one hand on the wall to prevent himself from falling. And so to his heated bedroom and to bed under a quilt with a hot-water bottle. He knows he has been indiscreet and will have to pay the price for his indiscretion on Christmas Day. What the hell does it matter? Christmas Eve comes only once every year. Christmas may or may not be merry, but Christmas Eve always is.

Christmas Day 2009. The morning is somewhat misty, as it is every Christmas morning in Delhi. The sun comes up in a clear blue sky. Dew on the lawn glistens for a while before it dries up. Church bells toll in different cathedrals and churches.

Christmas is of no significance in Baig's home. No doubt, like many Muslims, they revere *Eesa Masih* as a prophet, but attach no importance to his advent on earth. They also know that for Christians it is the Big Day—Bara Din. And many go to church at midnight to offer special namaaz, like some orthodox Muslims offer *tahajjud*. That's about it.

So on Christmas morning Baig, while sipping tea, announces to his Begum, 'Today is Bara Din.'

'I know,' replies Begum Sahiba. 'They enjoy themselves. Their bazaars are lit up many days earlier. They squander money buying gifts for each other, drink lots of wine, eat turkeys and puddings. Few bother to go to church to give thanks to their Maker.'

'So what's wrong with having a good time once or twice a year?' asks Baig.

'Janoo, what is wrong is to forget the One who gave you life and takes it back.'

'No one really knows very much about that,' says Baig and quotes a couplet:

All we know about life is about its middle
We know not its beginning, we know not its end.

'That sounds very clever, but in fact we do know Allah gave us life and Allah takes it back. He rewards those who do good deeds by sending them to Paradise and punishes the evil-doers by sending them to burn in hell. It's all written in our holy book. Every word of it is true because Allah himself conveyed it to our Prophet—peace be upon Him.'

Baig protests: 'Begum, why do you get so worked up when the subject of religion comes up?'

'I'll tell you why. Satan is on the rampage. Do you know that there are buses running in London with huge placards reading: "There may be no God, so why not relax?" What could be more shameless? If there was no God, there would be no human beings. Take that from me, because it is the truth.'

The argument comes to a close as the morning papers are delivered. Begum Sakina scans the headlines of an Urdu paper. Baig turns over the pages of the *Hindustan Times*. He spends a few minutes looking at pictures on the obit page to see if he knows anyone who has departed and puts the paper aside before asking his Begum to tell him what is happening in the world.

☙

On Christmas Day, Sharma resumes signing his name on greeting cards and putting addresses on envelopes. There is still a large number left but he has time as it is a postal holiday: he has to finish the job by next morning and post them himself. Because of this card business he has had to stay at home with his sister, which he finds tedious. So after breakfast he leaves for the India International Centre to read the papers. He sees the raunaq and enjoys the special menu prepared for the occasion. He tells his sister he has been invited by a friend to join him for lunch— which is not true. He will be back for his siesta and will go to Lodhi Gardens in the afternoon.

Boota wakes up with a hangover. His head throbs with pain. He takes a sip of tea and is overcome by nausea. He throws up in the washbasin. He can smell his dinner, wine and cognac in the vomit. He vomits three times, and all he ate the night before is washed down the sink. The throbbing in his head gets more painful. He wipes his face with a wet towel, swallows two pills of aspirin and returns to bed to sleep off the hangover. He falls into deep slumber and wakes up three hours later—exhausted, washed out, but minus the headache. He swears never to indulge himself in this reckless manner again. He tells

Bahadur to make him a Knorr packet soup and dry toast for lunch. It tastes delicious. He is back in bed and has another hour of sound sleep. Then he goes over newspaper headlines and hears the news on his TV. He has a quick shower, gets into his woollen kurta-salwar and proceeds to Lodhi Gardens.

ॐ

'So what's the big news on Bara Din? asks Baig.

'Nothing special,' replies his Begum. 'In Jharkhand that bearded fellow, Shibu Soren, who had been charged with bribery as well as murder, has once again been made chief minister. And you know how? The BJP has joined him. After all the talk of morality by the new BJP president, that fat Brahmin, Gadkari of Nagpur, has given his approval.'

'Talk of high morals is for the gullible public,' says Baig. 'Politics knows no morality. What else?'

'A lot about that police officer Rathore who molested fourteen-year-old Ruchika. And when her younger brother went to lodge a report against him, he was handcuffed and paraded in the bazaar. The poor girl took her life. It took nineteen years for the fellow to be sentenced to six months in jail and a fine of one thousand rupees. Gross miscarriage of justice. Now that there is a public uproar, and photographs of that Rathore coming out of court with a smirk on his face, he will get what he deserves. He should be flogged in public and sent to prison for life. Don't you agree?'

'These policewalas are like that—nothing new. Power goes to their heads and they do what they like. They should be taught a lesson they'll never forget.'

'And there is something about that eighty-three-year-old *boorha*, Narain Dutt Tiwari, governor of Andhra Pradesh, being caught on camera in bed with three prostitutes.' Begum Sahiba turns over the pages of her newspaper and says, 'Nothing else of much interest. The usual road accidents, thefts, rapes and all that.'

❧

Boota Singh is the last one to arrive at the Sunset Club meeting. Sharma gives him a withering look and says, 'You look like a corpse! What have you been up to?'

'Don't ask,' replies Boota. 'I've been very foolish; I forgot I am an old man now.'

'Drank too much?' asks Baig. 'Did you have a woman companion?'

'No such luck. Just recalled Christmas Eves of younger days.'

He quotes Ghalib:

Time has taken its toll on you and left you dead
Where are the frivolities of yesteryear?
Where has your youth fled?

'Well said,' comments Baig. 'One should know one's age and behave accordingly.'

That provokes Boota to quote an earlier couplet from the same verse:

The orgies of drinking all night are gone
Finished are the sweet dreams of the dawn.

Sharma remarks, 'Boota Singh is in a poetic mood of repentance.'

Boota can't stop himself:

Repentance oft before I swore
Was I sober when I swore?
Then came Spring hand in hand
And repentance threadbare it tore.

'Wah! Wah!' lauds Baig. 'If every binge turns you into a poet, then forget last night's overindulgence and let the wine flask and a cup always remain in front of you.'

Baig now seeks his friends' views on the news that had got his Begum so worked up that morning. 'Did you read about the retired DG Police of Haryana, Rathore, molesting a fourteen-year-old schoolgirl and compelling her to commit suicide? Boota, you are a great authority on sex aberrations, you must have something to say about Rathore.'

'I have,' replied Boota. 'All males are born badmashes. As soon as they see a woman, young or old, they want to ride her. And our police fellows are trained to be bullies; otherwise no one would be scared of them. I am sure this Rathore fellow is a bully, as well as a *jee hazoor*—a yes-sir—when it comes to important people. So he sucked up to chief ministers, they helped him win the police medal. Now he is in trouble, they pretend to know nothing of his private life. Haryana has a long tradition of lying chief ministers. As for Rathore, if it had not been for the girl's gutsy brother, who despite this fellow having him arrested, bullied, humiliated, beaten up, did not give up, the whole case would have been hushed up and forgotten.'

Baig protests: 'Bootaji, I am not a badmash. Sharmaji is not a badmash. You speak for yourself.'

'I am not a badmash either,' replies Boota. 'But can you deny that every male from the time he starts getting erections, begins to indulge in *badmashi*, looking for another boy's arse, or a woman's cunt, no matter who she is, to put it into? And the more important he becomes, the more he can get his way. Take the case of that fellow Michael Jackson, who died this summer. A great singer and dancer, worshipped by millions over the world. He was a laundebaaz, a sodomist and a catamite, and a child molester; a black man who had a nose job done, his hair straightened, and pretended to be a white woman. A total mix-up and yet hailed as one of the greatest of the great. And this golf champion Tiger Woods—another great black. He makes countless crores winning championships and through advertising. He lives in a palatial mansion, marries a pretty blonde Scandinavian, and has children through her. Then goes off his rocker, fucks dozens of blondes, crashes his car into a roadside hydrant. His teeth are smashed and he tells the world how to fuck up life.'

Boota continues, 'And look at Narain Dutt Tiwari. He must be quite a *tees maar khan*—a killer of thirty. He is eighty-three and has three women in bed to celebrate Christmas. At his age most men can't get an erection—or their erections which were once like the Qutub Minar made of solid stone, now look like the Leaning Tower of Pisa made of soft wax. I say, shabash—well done.'

Sharma responds, 'He is a Brahmin. Brahmins can do things which other castes can't.'

Boota shoots back: 'Panditji, you are also a Brahmin. Your sex exploits could be written behind a postage stamp.'

'You know nothing about my sex exploits as you call them,' retorts Sharma. 'In any case I have better things to occupy my mind than think of women.'

Baig intervenes, 'I am a Pathan, but I can barely look after one woman. And even her as an old companion. I

give full marks to Tiwari—he is a lusty Hero Number
One. I am amazed he has got so far in life despite his
preoccupation with women.'

'He has always been a *khushamdi tattoo*—a flattering pony,'
says Boota. In his days he was known as Sanjay's tattoo:

Main Narain Dutt Tiwari hoon,
Main Sanjay ki savaaree hoon
Na nar hoon na naari hoon
Indira ka pujaari hoon

Narain Dutt Tiwari am I
Sanjay's pony also am I
Neither male nor female am I
Indira Gandhi's worshipper am I.

All three have a hearty laugh: 'Wah bhai wah, Boota!
You have a good memory,' says Baig. 'I had forgotten
these lines long ago. I must recite them to my Begum.'

Sharma says in a grave tone, 'You people only think of
his lust for women. Does it not worry you what will
happen to our country if people at the top behave in this
reckless manner? What kind of example are people like
Tiwari setting?'

'Sharmaji, this is a lighter side to the drama. Women fall
for VIPs. You see how many working women fall for their
bosses. One boss goes, another comes and they switch
their affection to him. We have no such luck,' says Baig.

'How do you think Tiwari faces his wife and children? That is what I would like to know,' says Sharma. 'And he is also said to have a bastard son he now disowns. How does he face the boy's mother? These people have thick skins. They only think of their own pleasures and grabbing more power.'

'When the fellow resigned from the governorship—I am sure Sonia ordered him to resign—he said he was doing so on grounds of health. The next day he arrives in his hometown Dehra Dun to a pre-arranged welcome, and announces that all charges against him are false and he has no intention of retiring from politics. What do you make of a character like him?' says Baig.

'Why pick on Tiwari? An unruly cock has been the undoing of men much greater than him. It is not for nothing that Hindus worship the lingam,' says Boota.

Sharma's hackles rise. He admonishes Boota in stern tones: 'Boota, you understand nothing about religious symbolism. A lingam is not what you think it is. It is a symbol of creativity. All religions have symbols: Christians have the cross, Hindus have the letter Om, Muslims have the crescent moon, Sikhs have their *khanda-kirpan*. They revere them, not worship them. For that matter, you Sikhs have the five Ks. Tell me what possible religious significance the kachha—underwear—or *kangha*—comb—have?'

Baig intervenes, 'Let's not wrangle about religious matters. Love all human beings, says the Koran. But Muslims go on killing each other. Hardly a day passes when you don't hear about Sunnis throwing bombs on mosques and attacking Shia processions. And vice versa. I feel sick when I hear about it. I find religious disputes meaningless and petty. I share Ghalib's views: "I know the rewards of prayer and words of wisdom, but it is my nature to be indifferent towards them." Sex scandals are more my cup of tea.'

The sun goes down, it gets chilly and there is the dampness of dew in the air. Baig's servant puts a shawl on his master's shoulders and says, 'Sahib, it has got very cold. Let's get back home.' He helps his master get into his wheelchair. As Baig waves farewell to his friends, Sharma responds with another French phrase he knows: '*A demain*, which means, see you tomorrow.'

Back home, before Sharma can get down to clearing his Christmas mail, his sister asks, 'Was that Boota there this evening? His servant Bahadur told Pavan he was throwing up all morning, then drinking black coffee and swallowing pills to rid himself of his headache. He must have drunk like a *danger*—an ox—the evening before!'

'Yes, he was there, looking very ill but chirping away like a bulbul.'

Sharma is not looking forward to a dinner of daal-rice and egg bhujiya, which is what his sister is likely to give him. He asks sullenly, 'What are we having for dinner?'

'Omelette.'

Sharma makes a face. 'An omelette on Christmas Day?'

'I got a chocolate cake for dessert. If you wanted something special, why didn't you tell me in the morning?'

It puts Sharma in an even worse mood. 'I just want a tasty dinner and some variation now and then. That's not asking too much.'

It ruins the atmosphere. He gets down to his whisky, she to the TV. There is no talk between them. He is back to dealing with his mail till dinner is served.

∾

Baig tells his Begum of Boota's *sher-o-shairee*. 'The fellow has a good memory. He comes out with the right couplets to illustrate what he is saying. He drank too much last evening and was sick in the morning. So he was quoting Ghalib on the joys of drinking in one's youth and feeling sorry for his inability to continue doing so in old age.'

'That's what Ghalib is about: drink, women, loss of youth and death.'

Baig does not respond, and Sakina Begum continues, 'Janoo, am I wrong in thinking that most of our great poets were *randeebaaz*—whoremongers—and *sharabees*—

drunkards? Ghalib, the greatest of them, did not write a word in praise of his wife Umrao Begum who bore him half a dozen children, all of whom died in their infancy, but he composed an elegy for his low-caste mistress. And all his love poetry is addressed to prostitutes. Where else but in a brothel would he be asking a woman to open up during drink time, or would he take liberties with her on the excuse of being drunk? And where else but in a brothel would he have indulged in *dhaut-dhappa*—fisticuffs?'

Baig ponders over the question and replies, 'You may be right, but that does not detract from the greatness of his poetry. It was a gift given to him by Allah.'

Begum Sakina is silent for a while, then says, 'Well, your Boota really is a Rangeela Sardar. He must have been quite a womanizer in his youth.'

'He is good company. He spices his talk with anecdotes, quotations and improper language. One can never tell how much of what he says is true, but it doesn't matter. I enjoy listening to him. I can't say that about Sharma. I respect his learning but not his lectures.'

'It is a long time you three have been together. More than forty years, I think.'

'I've lost count. I don't even remember when and how we got together. For years I passed Boota and Sharma without a nod, all three of us walking at a brisk pace for our evening exercise. Then our paces got slower. I greeted them without knowing their names. Then Sharma and I began to use walking sticks and have servants follow us. Our walks became slower and we found ourselves sitting on the same bench, facing Bara Gumbad, talking about every subject on earth. People who come to Lodhi Gardens call it the Boorha Binch, meant exclusively for us three oldies.' Baig gives a big sigh and reclines in his chair. The maidservants sit on their haunches at his feet and begin to press his legs. His bearer brings his Scotch and soda on a silver tray. Baig helps himself to his drink. His Begum draws her dupatta over her nose and turns around to watch TV.

On New Year's Eve the three are sunning themselves sitting on the Boorha Binch, eyes closed and legs outstretched. They are not in a mood to talk. They yawn and take long breaths. Dabboo Three is fast asleep by his master's side. Baig's servants sleep on the lawn a few feet behind the bench. There are a lot of people in the park, some walking, others stretched out on the grass. Children run around. It is a peaceful, restful afternoon.

Baig yawns again and exclaims: 'Ya Allah, how quickly the year has gone by. It seems as if last New Year's Eve was just yesterday. Much happened in 2009. We should ponder over that.'

'Nothing special about 2009,' says Sharma. 'Bombs exploding in different places; prices of essential commodities going up and up; Naxalites killing policemen; policemen killing Naxalites and government spokesmen telling us all is well. India is shining, because the aam aadmi is happy. I am an aam aadmi. I am not happy with the way things are going.'

'Pandit, are you ever happy?' asks Boota. 'We had general elections in which the fundoos got a licking. For the first time we have a government of able ministers— not one of them accused of making illicit money. We are doing better than any of our neighbours. The scene is not so bleak as you make it out to be. See the brighter side of life.'

Baig agrees with Boota. 'We have to concede that despite widespread corruption the country has gone ahead in many fields. Instead of always criticizing the government, if the Opposition parties occasionally gave it a helping hand we could have done better.'

Boota again takes up against Sharma's pessimistic outlook. 'Panditji, you must have read in the morning papers that an Indian girl, Reeta Kaushal, reached the South Pole and planted the Indian flag there. Does it not make you feel proud of Indian women?'

'Brahmin,' says Sharma.

Boota flares up. 'Is that all you have to say—Brahmin? Indian girls have climbed Everest. I am not sure if any of them were Brahmins. And now we have the first woman president, the first woman speaker of the Lok Sabha and what's more she's Scheduled Caste. We have women cabinet ministers, chief ministers, governors of states, foreign secretary, commanders in the defence services, vice-chancellors of universities—some Brahmins, others not. Can you tell me of any other country which has done so much to uplift women to such heights?'

Sharma retorts: 'At the same time we continue to abort female foetuses, bury newborn baby girls. You should know because your Sikh Jats and Haryana Jats are the worst offenders in destroying females. Don't be carried away by all the government propaganda—take a realistic view of things as they are.'

❧

In Baig's home, New Year's Eve is no different from Christmas Eve. There is no celebration nor any special food. When Baig reminds his Begum that it is the last day of 2009, she says, 'I know; by the Christian calendar. We follow the Hijri. It is the 13th of Muharram. We don't celebrate it as New Year's Day.'

Boota celebrates New Year's Eve by ordering dinner from Claire Dutt, an Anglo-Indian who does a commendable job with anything she makes. This time she says, 'I'll make something new. Leave it to me.' Boota invites Sharma—he is always eager to eat tasty food and Boota is a generous host. They never invite Baig: he does not fit in in this kind of party.

Sharma arrives, walking stick in right hand, his servant Pavan holding his left hand, Dabboo Three waddling behind them. Pavan helps his master into an armchair facing Boota's, puts his walking stick behind him, and joins Boota's servant in the kitchen, which is the second warmest place in the flat.

'So ends another year,' says Sharma as he plugs in his hearing aid in his ears. 'I did not think I would last this long, did you?'

Boota answers by quoting Ghalib about the galloping pace of life and not having one's hands on the reins, then adds, 'But why discuss this gloomy topic on New Year's Eve? Single malt with soda or water?'

'Neat—single malt tastes best unadulterated.'

Boota pours two hefty pegs in cut-glass tumblers and adds soda and ice in his own glass. They raise their glasses, clink them and say, 'Cheers, Happy New Year to you.' Having said that, Sharma adds, 'There is nothing to be cheerful or happy about. When I think of my friends, not one of them besides you is alive today.'

'Well,' says Boota, 'the fact that we have outlived them is good enough reason to celebrate!' Then he recites Thomas Moore's nostalgic poem:

Oft in the stilly night
Ere slumber's chain has bound me
Fond memory brings the light
Of other days around me
The smiles, the tears
Of boyhood years,
The words of love then spoken
The eyes that shone,
Now dimmed and gone
The cheerful hearts now broken.

'There you are! Broken hearts have nothing to be cheerful about,' says Sharma.

Exactly at 8 p.m. Claire Dutt's man delivers dinner with the bill. The dessert is complimentary. Boota pays him in cash, adds a handsome tip and tells his servant to heat up the dinner and serve it in another half-hour. Boota pours a second round for his friend and himself. He uncorks a bottle of Barolo and puts it near the fireplace to bring it to room temperature.

Neither of them can recognize what the main dish is. It looks like pieces of chicken breast, corn and broccoli. It is delicious. Both have second helpings. The dessert is plum pudding. Boota pours some cognac on it and sets it on fire—a blue flame envelops the pudding. They have large helpings and there is enough left to last Boota for three more dinners.

The mixture of drinks and food makes both men a little groggy. It is well after 9 p.m., time for old men to retire before Dilliwalas begin to make their way to restaurants and hotels to begin their New Year's Eve celebrations. As Sharma gets unsteadily to his feet and grasps his walking stick, Boota comes out with one of his favourite quotes, from Walter Savage Landor:

I strove with none; for none was worth my strife;
Nature I loved, and next to Nature, Art;
I warm'd both hands before the fire of life;
It sinks, and I am ready to depart.

'So am I—in more ways than one. Cheers!' Sharma shouts, 'Pavan, chalo; Dabboo, chalo.' Pavan helps him up, and the three shuffle out of the room.

After Sharma leaves, Boota continues sitting in his armchair near the fireplace. His thoughts go back to his years in England. He is filled with nostalgia. It used to be so much fun—drinking, dancing, singing and flirting. As the midnight hour struck, the entire crowd would break into singing 'Auld Lang Syne'. They bade the year goodbye by embracing each other and kissing all the girls.

Indians tried to create the same kind of atmosphere in their elite clubs and five-star hotels. For many New Year's

Eves, Boota and his wife went to the Gymkhana Club or the Golf Club. They also drank a lot and danced a lot. At midnight, lights were switched off for a minute and you could kiss any woman who was willing to be kissed. After his wife died, Boota went to one or the other of the clubs. He drank steadily till midnight and invariably had a hangover on New Year's Day. The last time he went to the Golf Club, he drank more than usual and tried to dance the tango with a South Indian woman whom he knew slightly and had kissed on the cheeks. As the lights were switched off, he kissed the woman on her lips. She slapped him on the face and said angrily, 'How dare you!' and walked off. Boota returned home much chastened and kept muttering: 'Bitch, bitch. I'll never see her again.' Since then he has never been to a New Year's Eve party.

By 9.30 p.m., Boota is in bed with his hot-water bottle. At midnight he is woken up by the bursting of crackers and boys shouting on the streets. He knows 2009 is dead, 2010 has been born. He falls asleep.

The year 2009 is called the Year of the Blue Moon because in December it had two full moon nights, one on the 2nd and the other on New Year's Eve. It is a rare occurrence which most people believe is a good omen. But in December there was also a lunar eclipse which most people believe is a bad omen. So no one knows how 2010 will turn out: it's in the lap of the gods, if there are any.

13

THE SUNSET HOUR

We began our story on the 26th of January 2009, we should end it on the 26th of January 2010. Not much difference in the weather of the two Januarys. Bitterly cold and foggy in the mornings, pale sun which takes long to warm the chill out of one's bones. The well-off have electric radiators, log fires, whisky, quilts and hot-water bottles to keep them warm. The not-so-well-off lie on footpaths through the nights. Many succumb to the cold and are counted in the newspapers.

The New Year began on a sad note for both India and Pakistan. In Peshawar, a Talibani exploded a bomb at a volleyball match. He killed thirty-two spectators and maimed over seventy. And lost his life as well. When will this madness end? On the same day India lost its most famous wildlife protector, Billy Arjan Singh. He was ninety-two and lived alone in his bungalow in the midst of tigers, leopards and other wild beasts. None of them harmed him, because he had befriended them. A unique character, he was. Born in the Christian branch of the Kapurthala family, he was evidently impressed by the life of St Francis of Assisi and proved to the world that if you give love to animals and birds, they will give you as much love in return. There are not many of his kind living today.

On a cold, foggy morning arrived Sheikh Hasina, prime minister of Bangladesh, on an official visit. She was warmly received in Delhi. Relations between the two countries had cooled to near hostility after her father and other members of her family were shot dead by pro-Pakistan assassins. Her father, Sheikh Mujibur Rahman, affectionately called Banga Bandhu, was the founding father of independent Bangladesh. India had gone out of its way to help him, and the freedom fighters, Mukti Bahini, to inflict a humiliating defeat on the Pakistan army. Bangladesh and its rulers after Sheikh Mujibur Rahman showed gross ingratitude by siding with Pakistan in its disputes with India. Sheikh Hasina turned the tide in India's favour. There was good reason to give her a warm welcome.

Two days later, on the 12th of January, a violent earthquake devastated Haiti's principal city Port-au-Prince, taking a toll of over twenty thousand, one of the worst earthquakes in world history. What had the Haitians done to be punished like this? Where was Almighty and Merciful God?

Perhaps He had gone to Hardwar to have a holy dip in the icy-cold waters of the Holy Ganga during the Kumbh Mela. Was He washing away the sin He had committed in Haiti? As expected, there was a huge crowd at the Kumbh Mela, running into millions. But He saw to it that this time there was no stampede to take the lives of innocent people, as He was among them. In any event, He organized a solar eclipse to express His regrets for what He had done.

On the 17th died Jyoti Basu, ex-chief minister of West Bengal. He had been ailing for a long time, which gave many opportunities to leaders of the country to come and enquire about his health. They came in droves, from the prime minister down to chief ministers and other netas who longed to be photographed by his bedside. He had been chief minister for twenty-three long years. He did not do much for his state and let trade unions destroy many industries by going on strikes and gheraoing businessmen at their residences. But he managed to hang on to his post for a record time. The people of Kolkata gave him a grand funeral, ending with soldiers firing guns in the air and comrades giving him clenched-fist salutes.

Fog and cold continued day after day. It was particularly dense on the morning of the 24th, raising fears that it might ruin the spectacular parade on Republic Day. Many plane and rail services had to be cancelled. Fortunately, on the morning of Republic Day the fog lifted before 8 a.m., and the president of South Korea, who was the chief guest, saw with his own eyes what India is capable of doing to nations which cast their evil eyes on it.

We have strayed from our main topic. What happened to the Sunset Club? It met as usual on the afternoons of the 1st and 2nd of January. Its members discussed events of the first two days of the year.

On the 3rd morning, in Baig Manzil, everyone is up in time for the morning namaaz, awaiting the Nawab Sahib's loud announcement 'Ya Allah' as he yawns and stretches out his arms, to indicate that it's time for everyone to get down to his or her job. But no call is heard. Begum Sakina gets down to giving instructions for the day—she gives the menus for the afternoon and evening meals, doles out cash for meat, chicken and vegetables, and orders the other servants to get on with their daily chores. So passes half an hour.

Then Begum Sakina tells a maidservant to take tea and wake up the Nawab Sahib. She goes off with the tea tray. There are sounds of the tray and cups crashing on the floor, and the maidservant screams, *'Hai Allah, yeh kya ho gaya*—oh God, what's happened!' Begum Sakina and the servants run to the Nawab's bedroom. His eyes and mouth are half-open. He is dead. Begum Sakina wails, 'Barkoo, what is this? You have left me behind!' She beats her chest and slaps her forehead. The servants embrace each other and cry loudly. Truly had Ghalib spoken:

It is noise that turns a house into a home;
If it is not wailing for the dead,
It is songs of joy sung at a wedding

It is quite some time before Begum Sakina is able to control her emotions and get on with the job in hand. 'Inform all relatives and friends,' she orders. 'Also newspapers,' she adds. The servants get busy on the two mobile phones and the landline, giving the news to everyone they can think of.

Boota is in his cushioned chair in his heated bedroom. He has gone over the headlines of all the six newspapers he gets and is engrossed in solving crossword puzzles. His phone in the next room rings. He never answers telephone calls. It goes on ringing till Bahadur picks up the receiver and takes the message from the caller. He brings the cordless phone and says, 'It is somebody from Nawab Sahib's home.'

Boota takes the cordless. The voice at the other end asks, 'Is it Sardar Boota Singhji speaking?'

'Yes,' answers Boota, *'farmaaiyey*—speak.'

'Sahib, it is bad news. This morning Nawab Sahib became beloved of Allah.'

'What are you saying?' asks a very bewildered Boota. 'I was talking to him last evening. He was in perfect health.'

'Only Allah knows,' replies the servant. 'When a maidservant brought him his morning cup of tea, he was gone. She screamed loudly, "Hai Allah!" and all of us rushed to his bedroom. Begum Sahiba asked me to tell you that the funeral will take place at 3 p.m. He is to be buried in the family graveyard in Nizamuddin. Kindly inform Pandit Sharma.' His voice choked as he put down the phone.

Boota shuts his eyes. Tears roll down his cheeks into his beard. He sobs and more tears come dripping down. It takes him almost half an hour to compose himself. He realizes he will not be able to convey the news to Sharma on the phone. He scribbles a note and asks Bahadur to deliver it to Panditji. It reads: 'Just got a call from Baig's home. He died in his sleep early this morning. The funeral is at 3 p.m. Pick me up around 2.30 p.m.—Boota.'

At 2.30 p.m. Sharma's driver rings Boota's doorbell. Boota gets into Sharma's car. Sharma asks, 'What happened? He was okay last evening.'

'I don't know anything,' replies Boota. 'His servant only said that when a maidservant took him his morning cup of tea, he was dead.'

They fall silent. Outside Baig Manzil, many cars are parked. The gates are closed. Sharma and Boota get down and are let in. The front lawn is filled with men in skullcaps and salwar-kameez. A few are in Western dress. Sharma and Boota are escorted to the veranda where Begum Sahiba is receiving women who have come to condole. Neither of them has set eyes on Baig's wife before. She is a fair, plump woman who looks to be in her mid-seventies. Boota is reminded of the saying, 'Ruins proclaim the grandeur of the monument that was.' Her eyes are red with weeping but she looks in control of herself. Boota's tears begin to flow again and all he can do is wring his hands to indicate his bewilderment. Sharma delivers a short speech: 'We are much shocked by his sudden departure. A forty-year-old friendship has come to a sudden end. No one knows the ways of God.'

The Begum replies, '*Shukriya*—thanks. He talked about you both every evening when he returned from Lodhi Gardens. You need not wait for the *namaaz-e-janaza*—funeral prayers. It is kind of you to have called.'

Boota is unable to utter a word but his heart is full of grief. Begum Sahiba is touched by his grief.

On the lawn, men are lining up for funeral prayers. Sharma and Boota walk past them to Sharma's car. They drive back home without exchanging a word.

The next three days, as if by tacit agreement, neither of them goes to Lodhi Gardens. The Sunset Club would not be the same without Baig. Boota does a round of the lawn facing his flat. It is not much fun: as usual, boys and girls playing badminton and running around chasing balls, with their dogs running after them. Sharma spends his evenings going round Khan Market, peering into brightly lit shop windows. The market is perpetually being renovated. Heaps of bricks lying about force shoppers to avoid the pavements. There is no place for parking, so cars keep driving in and out of the entrance and exit gates. At places, footpaths are dug up to widen roads for the Commonwealth Games.

Sharma brings trouble on his own head. On the evening of the 10th of January 2010, as he is on his way back home, he stumbles over a large paving stone from the broken-up footpath and falls on the road. He is unable to get up as he has cracked his hip bone. Pavan drags him on to the pavement till he can get help. Shopkeepers come running to ask him if they can be of any assistance. Most of them know Sharma because he has been living in the neighbourhood for many years. A few minutes later, Sharma's nephew arrives in his car. He and Pavan lift Sharma and put him on the back seat. They pick up Sunita and drive to Malhotra's Nursing Home. He is examined by a couple of doctors. X-rays are taken and it is decided to operate on him next morning. Sharma is in acute pain all night and is unable to even turn in bed. Sunita, Pavan and his nephew spend the night in the nursing home. The next morning Sharma's nephew rings up Boota and tells him of the accident and where they are.

Boota immediately drives to the nursing home. Sharma is still in the operation theatre. An hour later, Sharma is brought back to the room, still under the influence of the anaesthetic given to him. He is groaning with pain. Boota sits by his side, holding his hand. Sharma's sister sits on the other side, holding the other hand. Sharma shakes off the numbness caused by the anaesthetic. His sister asks in a sharp tone: 'Who told you to go walking around Khan Market at night? See the result!'

A doctor comes in and asks, 'How are you feeling? The operation was successful. We have put your broken bones together. It will take some time for them to join properly.'

Boota speaks up: 'Doctor Sahib, why don't you give him a painkiller? He is in acute agony.'

The doctor gives him a withering look. 'I am going to do that. I know my job.'

Boota leaves Sharma's room at noon. 'See you tomorrow. You will be okay in a few days.'

Boota spends the next two days in the nursing home and reads out the news to Sharma from a couple of papers. He goes into details of sex scandals and the philandering of so-called godmen to cheer him up. Sharma seems to be in less pain and obviously on the mend. When no one besides Boota is in the room, Sharma smiles and says, 'Boota, you know what?'

'What?'

'You won't believe me. That Lakshmi, remember her? The one who wanted to marry me? She came this morning. She is married and has two children. There was no one else in the room. She sat on my bed and kissed me on the lips. Then undid her blouse and said, "Kiss me here," putting her breasts on my lips. Can you believe it!'

'You lucky bugger,' says Boota.

When the doctor comes on his round, Boota asks him as politely as he can, 'Doctor Sahib, when will you discharge Sharmaji?'

'As soon as we think he is fit to go home,' replies the doctor curtly.

'*Badtameez*—mannerless!' mumbles Boota as soon as the doctor leaves. 'I ask him a question politely, he barks back like a dog.'

'Don't mind him. He is a busy man. And has done a good job on me, I hope,' says Sharma.

The next afternoon Sharma is discharged and returns home. The doctor promises to visit him in a couple of days to see if he is doing well. Boota does not call on Sharma at home as it is full of his relations and friends.

On the afternoon of the 15th of January 2010, Boota is at home in his armchair, not sure whether or not to do a round of the lawn in front, or to do a couple of rounds of his back garden. Sharma's niece enters the room, sits down on the moorha beside his chair and takes his hand in hers. 'What's up?' he asks.

'I thought I'd come myself to tell you. Uncle died a couple of hours ago.'

Boota groans, 'No, no, no,' and breaks into sobs. He fails to put his emotions in words and just wrings his hands in despair as he sobs. Sharma's niece presses his hand, sits with him for ten minutes before leaving quietly.

Boota doesn't attend Sharma's funeral—just sits all day long staring at his walls lined with books. This goes on for a week. He reads Sharma's obituaries in different papers. Tributes are paid to him by the prime minister and other leaders. There is also an announcement of a prayer meeting in the Chinmayanand Hall. He decides not to go for it as he knows he will make a fool of himself.

He argues with himself. He must come to terms with the realities of life—and death. Both Baig and Sharma had had good innings and lived longer than most Indians do. He is much the same age. His turn will come soon. When? No one knows.

He opens his telephone book and turns over its pages from A to Z. Every second or third entry has a line drawn down it, and beneath it one line saying D. 1981, D. 1985, D. 1987 and so on. He turns back to B, draws a line down Baig, Barkatullah and writes D. 3.1.2010; then turns to S and crosses out Sharma, Preetam and writes D. 15.1.2010. He also has his own name in the telephone book—not because he is in his dotage, but for anyone who asks for his telephone number. Against his own name he adds:

D. date?

month?

year?

Boota pulls himself out of his mood of despondency. It is the morning of Republic Day 2010. He watches the parade on TV. The parade is much the same as it was last year, and the years before it.

In the afternoon he goes to Lodhi Gardens. There is quite a crowd of people picnicking. The Boorha Binch is unoccupied. He sits down and gazes at the Bara Gumbad.

A gardener distracts his attention: 'Sardar Sahib, you have not been seen for some days. And where are your friends?'

'Gone up,' replies Boota, raising his hands towards the sky.

The gardener understands the gesture: '*Dono*—both of them? I am sorry to hear that.'

Boota again raises his hand and says, 'Bhai, who knows the ways of God?'

The gardener agrees: 'Haan, no one knows what Bhagwan wills.'

Boota returns to gazing at the Bara Gumbad. It does resemble the fully rounded bosom of a young woman.

TAMAAM SHUD

green leaves'—are from *The Golden Tradition: An Anthology of Urdu Poetry* translated and edited by Ahmed Ali.

The poems by Kalidas on page 151 have been translated by Arthur W. Ryder.

Also by Khushwant Singh

ABSOLUTE KHUSHWANT: THE LOW-DOWN ON LIFE, DEATH AND MOST THINGS IN-BETWEEN

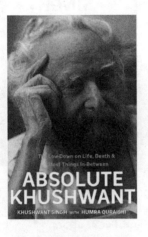

'I would like to be remembered as someone who made people smile.'

In *Absolute Khushwant*, India's grand old man of letters tells us about his life, his loves and his work. He writes on happiness, faith and honesty. And, for the first time, about his successes and failures, his strengths and weaknesses, his highs and lows. He tells us what makes him tick and the secret of his longevity; he confesses his deepest fears and what he holds dear. He writes about sex, marriage, worship and death; the people he's admired and detested. With personal anecdotes and rare photographs, *Absolute Khushwant* is uncompromising, moving, and straight from the heart.

'This is vintage Khushwant—charming and forthright'
—*The Telegraph*

Non-fiction
Rs 250

CLASSIC KHUSHWANT SINGH

This omnibus edition brings together all of Singh's novels—four classics of modern Indian literature: *Train to Pakistan, I Shall Not Hear the Nightingale, Delhi* and *Burial at Sea*.

First published in 1956, *Train to Pakistan* is a timeless classic of modern Indian fiction.

I Shall Not Hear the Nightingale is widely acclaimed as Khushwant Singh's finest novel.

Delhi is Khushwant Singh's bawdy, irreverent magnum opus, about an ageing reprobate who travels through time, space and history to 'discover' his beloved city.

Comic, tender and erotic by turns, *Burial at Sea* is vintage Khushwant Singh.

Fiction Omnibus
Rs 499

THE PORTRAIT OF A LADY:
COLLECTED STORIES

'A Khushwant Singh short story is not flamboyant but modest, restrained, well-crafted . . . perhaps his greatest gift as a writer is a wonderful particularity of description'—*London* magazine

Khushwant Singh first established his reputation as a writer through the short story. His stories—wry, poignant, erotic and, above all, human—bear testimony to his remarkable range and his ability to create an unforgettable world.

Spanning over half a century, this volume contains all the short stories Khushwant Singh has ever written, including the delightfully tongue-in-cheek 'The Maharani of Chootiapuram', written in 2008.

'Khushwant's stories enthrall . . . [He has] an ability akin to that of Somerset Maugham . . . the ability to entertain intelligently'—*India Today*

'His stories are better than [those of] any Indian writing in English'—*Times of India*

'*The Collected Short Stories* leaves the readers in a delightful, inebriated trance'—*Sunday Chronicle*

Fiction
Rs 350